W9-AMA-335

"Mallory, I can't keep you safe unless you're honest with me.

"If you tell me the truth, I'll make sure the D.A. knows how you cooperated with our investigation."

"What do you mean you'll convince the D.A. I've cooperated with the investigation? I'm not involved in anything illegal. I'm the victim here. Caruso's thug followed me to my sister's town house and tried to kill me!"

"Yeah, maybe," Jonah said, and his calm voice only fuelled her annoyance. "But just a few hours ago I was informed that Wasserman's body was found in an alley not far from your condo, and your fingerprints are on the knife in his belly. The M.E. has deemed his death a homicide. As a result, there's a warrant for your arrest."

"I swear to you, Jonah, I didn't kill him. Don't you see? I'm being framed for murder!"

Jonah's mouth tightened, but he didn't say anything. And she realized that Jonah Stewart hadn't come to Crystal Lake just to help find her twin. He'd come to take her back to Milwaukee.

To arrest her for a crime she didn't commit.

Books by Laura Scott

Love Inspired Suspense

The Thanksgiving Target
Secret Agent Father
The Christmas Rescue
Lawman-in-Charge
Proof of Life
Identity Crisis
Twin Peril

LAURA SCOTT

grew up reading faith-based romance books by Grace Livingston Hill, but as much as she loved the stories, she longed for a bit more mystery and suspense. She is honored to write for the Love Inspired Suspense line, where a reader can find a heartwarming journey of faith amid the thrilling danger.

Laura lives with her husband of twenty-five years and has two children, a daughter and a son, who are both in college. She works as a critical-care nurse during the day at a large level-one trauma center in Milwaukee, Wisconsin, and spends her spare time writing romance.

Please visit Laura at www.laurascottbooks.com, as she loves to hear from her readers.

TWIN PERIL

Laura Scott

Love Inspired

If you purchased this book without a cover you should be aware
that this book is stolen property. It was reported as "unsold and
destroyed" to the publisher, and neither the author nor the
publisher has received any payment for this "stripped book."

Recycling programs
for this product may
not exist in your area.

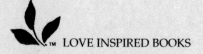 LOVE INSPIRED BOOKS

ISBN-13: 978-0-373-08323-7

TWIN PERIL

Copyright © 2012 by Laura Iding

All rights reserved. Except for use in any review, the reproduction
or utilization of this work in whole or in part in any form by any
electronic, mechanical or other means, now known or hereafter
invented, including xerography, photocopying and recording, or in
any information storage or retrieval system, is forbidden without
the written permission of the editorial office, Love Inspired Books,
233 Broadway, New York, NY 10279 U.S.A.

This is a work of fiction. Names, characters, places and incidents are
either the product of the author's imagination or are used fictitiously, and
any resemblance to actual persons, living or dead, business establishments,
events or locales is entirely coincidental.

This edition published by arrangement with Love Inspired Books.

® and TM are trademarks of Love Inspired Books, used under license.
Trademarks indicated with ® are registered in the United States Patent
and Trademark Office, the Canadian Trade Marks Office and in other
countries.

www.LoveInspiredBooks.com

Printed in U.S.A.

All the prophets testify about Him,
that everyone who believes in Him
receives forgiveness of sins through His name.
—*Acts* 10:43

This book is dedicated to Pam Hopkins
with deep appreciation for your ongoing support.

ONE

Mallory Roth awoke with a start, her heart thundering against her ribs in terror.

Had she imagined the noise?

The interior of her uncle Henry's cabin was shrouded with darkness. It was nestled in the woods in central Wisconsin with the back porch overlooking the town of Crystal Lake. The trees blocked any light from the moon, and in the darkness, she strained to listen.

Just when she figured she had let her imagination run wild, she heard it again—a low creak of the wooden floorboards from the main living area.

Her pulse surged into triple digits.

There was no time to waste. Anthony Caruso had found her.

She sucked in a quick breath and swung her legs over the edge of the bed, rolling into an upright position. She knew only too well that whoever was out there intended to silence her forever. As quietly as possible, she dragged a sweatshirt over her head and jammed her feet into running shoes. She picked up the thick stick from where she'd left it propped in the corner next to her bed, tightly grasping the only weapon she possessed.

Another muffled sound came from the other room. Closer. She imagined the intruder stealthily making his way toward the bedroom.

For half a second, she considered waiting for him behind the door so she could hit the back of his head. But then her self-defense training kicked in. Running away from an attack, if at all possible, was better than staying to fight. Weapons were all too often used against the victim.

She'd been lucky to escape the last man Caruso had sent after her with nothing more serious than a cut on her arm.

Looping her purse over her head so that it lay across her chest, leaving her arms free, she crossed the room and slid the window frame upward. She winced when the window gave a small groan. She'd already removed the screen in case she needed to use this window as her escape route. She quickly threw her leg over the threshold, stick in hand as she ducked through the opening.

The door to her bedroom burst open, and she turned in time to catch a glimpse of a tall man in black with a matching ski mask covering his face. She ran.

Dressed in dark clothing, she blended into the trees as she pulled up the hood of her sweatshirt to cover her blond hair. She ducked under low-hanging branches, making her way through the woods toward the highway. Trees and thick brush lined the highway on both sides, and her closest neighbor was located just a half mile south of the cabin.

She had to stay hidden long enough to get to the Andersons.

She could hear Caruso's thug swiping at branches and hitting trees as he followed behind her. Stark fear coated her throat.

The brush in the woods became less dense, and she could just barely make out the road. The guy behind her was closing in, and she pushed herself to go faster. But the moment she broke free of the woods, strong arms reached out to grab her. The shock of finding someone there waiting for her caused her to drop her weapon.

She'd run straight into a trap!

She tried to scream but the man clamped his hand over her mouth. "Don't," he whispered. "I'm a cop. If you want to stay alive, Mallory, come with me."

A cop? Or a partner to the guy in the black ski mask? Or both? She didn't know who to trust. The sound of the ski-masked thug crashing through the woods behind her helped make up her mind. She barely had time to pick up the stick from the ground before the cop dragged her down the road toward the car he'd parked along the side of the highway. She also noticed a large black truck parked across the street.

Pop! Pop!

"Keep your head down!" the cop yelled, yanking open the passenger-side door and shoving her inside. More popping sounds peppered the air as he ducked and ran around to the driver's side.

She barely had time to strap on her seat belt before her rescuer cranked the engine and floored the gas. He peeled away, her heart lodging in her throat as they careened down the highway.

Gripping the handrail with white-knuckled fingers, Mallory tried to find her voice as the cop drove through the night like a madman, taking the sharp curves in the highway at breakneck speed. She glanced over her shoulder to see the headlights dropping farther behind. The cop changed directions as often as possible in order to lose the truck.

She should have been reassured by his ability to evade the man behind them but she wasn't. Her teeth chattered and her body began to shake. She recognized the aftereffects of shock from the last time she'd narrowly escaped Caruso's thug.

She closed her mind against the memory of the bloody room in her twin sister's town house as she struggled to breathe.

The guy in the ski mask wasn't the same guy as before. He was tall and broad-shouldered compared to the shorter, stockier guy she'd taken down in Alyssa's town house just a few days ago. When her rescuer slowed his break-neck speed, she glanced back, relieved to see there were no longer any head-lights following them.

"Who are you?" she finally asked. "How did you find me?"

He didn't take his eyes off the road as he tossed a small leather case in her lap. She opened it and was slightly reassured when she saw the shiny metal glint of his badge. At least it looked real enough.

"My name is Jonah Stewart and I'm a detective with the Milwaukee Police Department." There was a long pause, before he added, "Your sister, Alyssa, sent me to find you."

Jonah didn't slow down until he was a good fifteen miles outside of town. And even then, he maintained a decent clip, pushing the posted speed limit, carefully watching the rearview mirror to make sure the guy in the black truck hadn't found them. When he was reasonably sure they were safe, he unclenched his fingers from their death grip on the steering wheel.

That had been way too close. If he'd arrived a minute later, he might have lost Mallory for good. When he'd gotten to the cabin just after midnight, he'd noticed the black truck and grown suspicious. Just as he started making his way down the driveway toward the cabin, he'd heard someone running through the woods. It only took a minute to rule out a four-legged animal—he'd heard the distinct sound of two people. He'd braced for the worst and been immensely relieved when Mallory had raced out of the woods first, apparently unharmed, just in the nick of time.

"Did you get a good look at him?" he asked in a gruff tone.

"No." She slowly shook her head. "His

face was covered by a ski mask. But why were you waiting on the road for me after midnight? You claim Alyssa sent you, but I know her and she would have come to meet me herself."

"Alyssa did send me. How else do you think I knew about the cabin? She also told me your uncle Henry is really your mother's cousin, and he hadn't been up here in a long time because he recently had a stroke." He hoped the additional information would reassure her that he was on the right side of the law.

"Yes," she admitted. "That's true."

"I found the place a few minutes before you came out of the woods." He sent a silent prayer of thanks, knowing God had been watching out for the both of them. "Alyssa didn't come herself because we didn't even know for sure you were here."

Mallory's scowl deepened. "What do you mean she didn't know? I left a message on her cell phone. I told her to come to the place she least expected to find me. As kids, we had to stay at the cabin for two weeks in the summer while our parents took an Alaskan cruise. Alyssa loved it, but I hated every minute. Do you realize I spent the last few days in a place with no indoor plumbing?"

For the first time in a long while, he was tempted to smile. He could well imagine how a cabin on a lake with an outhouse was not Mallory's idea of fun.

"Alyssa lost her cell phone and must not have picked up her messages. And the other reason she didn't come is she tore the ligaments and tendons in her ankle pretty bad. I convinced her that she'd only slow us down and she agreed I could protect you better by myself. She's scheduled for surgery later this week."

That news made Mallory sit up in her seat. "Surgery? What happened to her?"

"It's a long story." He continued to drive, deciding he wasn't stopping anywhere for a long time—maybe not even until daylight. "Several days ago Alyssa fell and hit her head. When she woke up, she had amnesia. Alyssa's boyfriend, Gage, thought she was you. They asked for my help because someone was trying to kill them. Don't worry, they're safe now. And once Alyssa's memory started to return, we realized you were missing and in possible danger. That's when we began searching for you." He glanced at her expectantly.

"Are you sure they're all right?"

"I promise they're fine," Jonah assured her.

"Then what happened to her ankle?" Mallory asked.

Was she really worried about her sister? Or was she simply asking more questions to put off telling him the truth? He wanted to believe the former, but his instincts warned him not to trust her too easily. He'd been burned by an apparent victim before.

"According to Gage, they had to climb out of a warehouse window and drop down to the ground, about ten feet. She landed hard on her ankle. Frankly, we were both surprised she hadn't broken it." He turned his attention back to the road, slowing down since they were approaching a small town.

"Are we stopping here?" Mallory asked.

"No."

"Why not?" she demanded. "How do I know I can really trust you? Let me out. I want to talk to Alyssa."

He stifled a heavy sigh. "Be reasonable. It's one o'clock in the morning."

"Reasonable?" Her voice rose a few decibels and he tried not to wince. "A man in a ski mask broke into my uncle's cabin to kill me. And suddenly you're conveniently waiting for me when I run out of the woods? Don't you dare accuse me of being unreasonable."

He held up his hand in surrender.

Good thing the rental car didn't need gas—he didn't doubt that Mallory would bolt the first chance she was given. He'd already saved her from the guy in the ski mask, so why was she so uptight?

"If you want to call your sister, go ahead. But the only number I have is Gage's cell." He tossed his phone into her lap.

She picked it up and grimaced. "Gage doesn't exactly like me," she said as she scrolled through the contact list. "How do you know him?"

"Gage and I went to high school together. Both he and Alyssa have been worried sick about you," Jonah added. He had been worried, too, mostly because he believed Mallory was the key to solving the case. Just a little over a week ago he and Gage had uncovered a money-laundering scheme that involved a man named Hugh Jefferson. Jonah had also been betrayed by a cop who'd tried to kill him. Soon he'd discovered that

Jefferson had been searching for Mallory, who'd disappeared.

Now that he'd found Mallory, he wanted to know exactly why she'd been hiding at the cabin. And why Jefferson had wanted to find her. All along they'd suspected there was a man higher up the chain of command, the one truly in charge of the money-laundering scheme. He was convinced Mallory knew the identity of that man, or at least someone working for him. Why else would Jefferson want to know where she was?

Mallory held the phone up to her ear. After several rings, the call went into voice mail. There was the faintest tremble in her voice as she spoke. "Gage? It's Mallory. Will you please have Alyssa call this number as soon as you can? Thanks."

She ended the call but kept a tight hold on the phone, as if waiting for her sister's return call. In the darkness, he was able to see the glitter of tears in her eyes. His gut clenched and he tightened his grip on the steering wheel. The last thing he needed was for her to break down.

"Look, I'm sorry. I understand you've been traumatized by everything that's happened. But, Mallory, I am a cop. And I promise I'll keep you safe."

A tense silence stretched between them. She sniffled loudly and swiped at her eyes. When her chin came up again, he almost smiled, impressed by her ability to pull herself together. Mallory was obviously a lot tougher than she looked. "You better. It's only fair to warn you, I have a black belt in Tae Kwon Do, and besides, I can call 9-1-1."

When she actually punched in the buttons, prepared to make the call, he reached over to take his phone back. She didn't let go. In the brief tussle, she brushed her arm against the side of his chest.

"What is this? Are you bleeding?" She stared in horror at the stain on her arm.

He glanced down in surprise, feeling the dampness against his shirt. It wasn't easy to see in the darkness, but he could feel blood oozing through the dressing along the right side of his chest.

"Yuck. I faint at the sight of blood." She rummaged through her purse, pulled out a small packet of wipes and cleaned the stain from her arm before glancing over to frown at him. "Are you sure you're okay? Were you hit by a bullet back there?" The concern in her eyes was nice even though he didn't deserve it. He wasn't here just to save her life—he was here to close his case.

"No, I'm fine." He realized the fresh surgical incision located along his rib cage was throbbing painfully. There was ibuprofen in his duffel bag, which was all he was willing to take. "It's just an old injury that must have opened up a bit."

"We'll have to stop at a drugstore and get some bandages," she murmured.

"Too bad I'm not Alyssa—you could probably use a nurse." She made a face as she placed a hand over her stomach. "I really am not much help when it comes to blood."

He gave a brief nod, even though he had no intention of stopping at a drugstore anytime soon. Right now, his reopened wound was the least of his worries.

First he needed to find a safe haven, somewhere they could stay for the next twenty-four hours. And then he needed to figure out a way to make Mallory trust him enough to tell him the identity of the man who was in charge of the money-laundering operation that had almost gotten them all killed.

Mallory sensed there was far more to the story regarding how Alyssa was injured than Jonah Stewart was telling her. But as much as she wanted to keep after him, she couldn't fight the wave of exhaustion washing over her, the adrenaline crash hitting hard. She wished she could talk to Alyssa.

She supposed it was logical that Gage wouldn't answer the phone in the middle of the night. And if Alyssa really had lost her cell phone, then there was nothing more she could do except wait until morning. She wondered how Gage and Alyssa were getting along. Jonah had made it sound as if they were a couple saying they were both worried about her. But Mallory knew better than to think Gage was worried—she could only hope he wouldn't let his personal feelings toward her get in the way of responding to her voice-mail message.

Back when Gage and Alyssa had started dating, she hadn't trusted Gage's feelings, especially the way he'd proposed so quickly. She'd shamelessly flirted with him as a way to test his feelings because, in her experience, men usually went for the easy, no-strings-attached type of relationship. But he'd surprised her by instantly shutting her down. He had claimed to love Alyssa, although just a short month later, she had returned his engagement ring.

Mallory suspected Alyssa still harbored deep feelings for Gage Drummond.

Since thinking about her past—and the way she'd messed up one relationship after another—was depressing, she concentrated on the present. Glancing over at Jonah, she focused on his wound. It wasn't easy to see the stain on his navy T-shirt, but she could tell the damp spot was spreading.

"Jonah, what happened? Why would an old wound bleed like that?"

"I had surgery about a week ago, and a few of the stitches must have popped open."

"What happened? Were you injured on the job?"

He clenched his jaw. "I was stabbed by

a dirty cop Gage and I discovered was working for Hugh Jefferson."

Mallory twisted her fingers together nervously. The architectural firm she worked for had been awarded the design contract for the Jefferson Project— fancy high-rise condos overlooking the Milwaukee River. She was the firm's interior designer, and her boss, Rick Meyers, was the one who'd introduced her to Anthony Caruso.

Caruso had talked often to Hugh Jefferson. The mere memory of what she'd overheard made her stomach roll with nausea. "What are you saying? That you have proof Jefferson was involved with illegal activities?"

"Yeah. We have proof of how he was involved in a money-laundering scheme. But now he's dead."

Her mouth dropped open in shock. Hugh Jefferson was dead? "Are you sure all this happened while I was making my way to the cabin?" She hated thinking she'd left Alyssa in danger.

"I'm sure." Jonah's tone was terse. "Jefferson's yacht caught on fire, and while Gage and Alyssa managed to escape, he and his cohorts didn't. All three of them died—Aaron Crane, the dirty cop, Hugh Jefferson and Eric Holden, the newly elected Milwaukee mayor. Well, technically, Holden died before he could be sworn into office."

She was disappointed that he hadn't mentioned Caruso. Listening to Jonah talk about the Jefferson Project confirmed that everything she'd suspected all along was true. There hadn't been some horrible mistake. Caruso really had sent that thug to kill her at Alyssa's town house, hoping to silence her forever. And then Caruso had found her again, at Uncle Henry's cabin. She licked her suddenly dry lips. "I'm relieved to know Alyssa and Gage escaped. But why were they even on the yacht in the first place? What possessed Gage to put Alyssa in danger?"

"Gage didn't put her in danger on purpose. In fact, he went to great lengths to keep her safe. But we didn't know exactly who she was running from, because of her amnesia."

She rubbed her temples, trying to make sense of what Jonah was saying. "I was the one they wanted to silence." She felt sick at the thought she'd inadvertently put Alyssa in danger. "They must have thought she was me."

"No, it wasn't that," Jonah said reassuringly. "Alyssa was working in the trauma room the night Councilman Schaefer was brought in with his stab wound. He told Alyssa that Jefferson was responsible. She believed him and reported the crime to Officer Crane, who happened to be working for Jefferson. He tried to kill her. More than once. If not for Gage's help, he might have succeeded."

Mallory shook her head, unable to process what he was saying. Wave after wave of regret battered her. She'd been so worried about her own well-being, especially after Wasserman followed her to Alyssa's town house, that she'd never considered her sister might be in just as much danger. She'd left the urgent message—assuming Alyssa would drop everything to come out to meet her—then ditched her phone, worried that Caruso had the means to track it. If only she and Alyssa had been able to talk to each other. They could have disappeared together.

"So now, Mallory, it's your turn. We know why Alyssa was in danger, but we don't know what happened to you. Did you stumble onto something you shouldn't have? Did you find out about the money- laundering scheme?"

"I don't even know what money laundering is." She kept her tone even with an effort.

"It's taking money received from illegal activities and putting it into legal activities," he explained, not willing to be distracted from his purpose. "You left a lot of blood on the floor of Alyssa's town house, along with a blood-stained blouse."

She shivered, remembering that night all too clearly.

"Mallory, are you listening to me? I can't keep you safe unless you're honest with me. Tell me the name of the man you're running from. If you do, I'll make sure the D.A. knows you cooperated with our investigation."

She snapped her head up to glare at him. A flash of anger blurred her vision, forcing her to wrestle it back to maintain control.

"What do you mean you'll convince the D.A. I've cooperated with the investigation? I'm not involved in anything illegal. I'm the victim here. Caruso's thug, a guy named Kent Wasserman, followed me to Alyssa's town house and tried to kill me!"

"Yeah, maybe," Jonah said, his calm voice only fueling her annoyance. "But just a few hours ago, I was informed that Wasserman's body was found in an alley not far from your condo, and your fingerprints are on the knife in his belly. The ME has deemed his death a homicide. As a result, there's a warrant for your arrest."

She couldn't have been more surprised if the car had sprouted wings to fly. How could there possibly be a warrant out for her arrest? He was the one who'd tried to kill her! She'd fought with Wasserman, sure, but only in self-defense. She'd barely escaped. And she didn't touch the knife.

At least, not that she remembered.

"I didn't kill him," she whispered, the images she'd tried to forget crowding in her mind. Somehow, someway, she had to make him believe her. "I swear to you, Jonah, I didn't kill him. Don't you see? I'm being framed for murder!"

Jonah's mouth tightened, but he didn't say anything. And that was when she realized that Jonah Stewart hadn't just come to Crystal Lake to help find her. He'd come to take her back to Milwaukee.

To arrest her for a crime she didn't commit.

TWO

"Jonah, please. You have to believe me. I didn't kill him!" Mallory fought to control the fear that began to constrict her throat.

"I guess it's possible you're being framed," Jonah said slowly, in a tone laced with doubt. "But we'd have to prove it, which isn't going to be easy. You have to tell me everything, Mallory, from the very beginning. I can't help you if you hold back on me."

For a moment she stared through the darkness at the trees passing in a blur outside her passenger-side window. She didn't know if she could trust Jonah. What if she told him what she knew and he still arrested her? Caruso was a powerful man—she had no doubt he'd find a way to kill her even if she happened to be in jail. Yet if she didn't tell him, Jonah would take her back to Milwaukee and arrest her for sure.

A no-win situation, either way.

She took a deep breath and then let it out slowly. "I started dating Anthony Caruso a few months ago," she admitted, avoiding his gaze.

"Anthony Caruso?" Jonah interrupted with a frown. "Who's he?"

"He's an Illinois senator. I'm not normally into the political scene, but when I met him, I liked him. He told me he was providing Hugh Jefferson with capital for his condo project."

At the time, dating him had seemed harmless. Caruso had been older than most of the men she'd dated—thirty-nine to her twenty-seven—but he'd been charming so she'd figured, why not? Looking back, she wondered how she could have been so stupid.

"An Illinois senator," Jonah repeated under his breath, as if he couldn't believe it. "I recognize his name now. It's been all over the news. He's a big deal in Washington. Exactly how did you meet him?"

"My boss, Rick Meyer, introduced me to him at one of the meetings about the Jefferson Project." She glanced away, not wanting to see the censure in his eyes. "I— Things moved pretty fast. He literally swept me off my feet. Bought me gifts, took me to fancy restaurants and even flew me to New York to see a Broadway show." She felt like an idiot now, knowing she'd been blinded by the wealth. And power. Anthony Caruso wielded a lot of power—more than she could have possibly suspected. "I never, in a million years, suspected he would get involved with anything illegal."

She forced herself to look at Jonah. Sure enough, his eyebrows levered upward in surprise. "Caruso himself is involved? Seriously? Are you absolutely certain?"

He didn't believe her, and that hurt. Why didn't anyone take her seriously? She tilted her chin stubbornly. "Yes, I'm sure. I was leaving his office suite in the hotel after we'd had lunch but I forgot my purse. I went back in quietly so I wouldn't disturb him. I saw him standing out on his terrace by himself, talking on his cell. He sounded very angry. I paused and overheard him telling the person on the other end of the line to do whatever was necessary to make sure the condo project went forward as planned because he had too much riding on it."

"That statement isn't necessarily incriminating," Jonah pointed out. "Could be interpreted as having money on the line, which isn't illegal. Anyone would be upset with losing money on a business deal."

"I know. But then he said, 'My sources

tell me Schaefer was alive when he hit the E.R., so you better make sure our guy on the inside convinces the public his death was the result of gang violence.'" She remembered how horrified she'd felt in that moment, realizing the senator was actually discussing how to cover up a murder. "I retraced my steps, trying to sneak away, but I think he must have heard me. I caught a glimpse of his face as he came in from the terrace just as I closed the door behind me. I ran down the hall and avoided the elevator, choosing the stairs instead. I managed to get out of the building, but I couldn't go home. I kept calling Alyssa's place, but she didn't pick up. I eventually went to her town house, using my key to get in. I had this crazy idea of borrowing her identity, but then I heard someone at the door and assumed it was my sister. Kent Wasserman barged in, holding a knife. We'd briefly met a few weeks earlier through Anthony. I was shocked to see him at Alyssa's and knew he must have followed me. He lunged but I managed to get away, taking him down in the process. He fell on his knife."

"You took him down?" Doubt radiated from his tone.

She narrowed her gaze. "Try me." She didn't bother explaining she'd been training in martial arts since her senior year in high school—specifically, since the night of the assault that had changed her life forever. She had absolutely no intention of explaining the private horror of her past to Jonah.

Besides, her past was old news. She'd moved beyond the assault, and she'd get herself out of this mess, as well. If necessary, she'd figure out something on her own. But she wasn't going to allow any man to hold her helpless ever again. That included all of the thugs Caruso sent out after her.

And Jonah Stewart, who was perhaps the most dangerous of all.

* * *

Jonah tried to mask his surprise. First, he found it hard to believe a state senator could actually be calling the shots in the Jefferson Project. And then of course there was the rest of Mallory's story. Including the part where she claimed to have a black belt in Tae Kwon Do. But she didn't hedge the way people sometimes did when they were lying, and he found himself believing her.

"That's a very serious allegation, Mallory. You'd better be sure about this. Anthony Caruso carries a lot of weight on Capitol Hill. There's been talk about him being a candidate for vice president, or even for the presidency itself in a few years. I don't think many people are going to believe your word over his."

"I know." She twisted her hands together in a nervous gesture. "That's the reason I ran. But I promise you, I'm not lying about this. I know what I heard."

"I believe you. But we need proof,

Mallory. If we're accusing a state senator of being involved, we need hard-core proof."

"I know," she murmured. Her face was grim and she sighed heavily. "Up until that point, I had no idea Anthony was involved in anything shady. I'd been dating him for almost a month and I never heard so much as an inkling of anything dangerous. It was a total fluke that I heard that snippet of his conversation at all. But I knew Councilman Schaefer had been stabbed so it didn't take much to put two and two together."

Jonah nodded, discovering he didn't particularly care to hear about how she'd dated the guy.

Not that Mallory's personal life was any of his concern.

He told himself to get a grip. "Okay, so you left Alyssa's town house after being attacked by Wasserman and escaped to Crystal Lake. Then what?"

She lifted one shoulder in a helpless

shrug. "Then nothing. I left Alyssa a message to meet me and hunkered down to wait."

"Anything out of the ordinary happen before tonight?" he persisted. "Anything at all to indicate Caruso had found you?"

"No. Not until I heard the guy sneaking through the cabin."

If nothing else, the guy in the ski mask helped reinforce her story about overhearing Caruso's conversation. There was no other reason for Caruso to try to kill her.

Unless there was far more to the story than she was telling him.

He didn't want to think Mallory may have been a part of the crime, but he couldn't totally discount the idea, either.

"Why didn't you go to the police with your story?"

In the darkness he saw her scowl. "Because Anthony referred to *our guy on the inside,* making it difficult to know who to trust. Besides, I was waiting for

Alyssa to meet me at the cabin. I guess I hoped we'd work together to figure out the next step."

Grudgingly, he had to admit her instincts were right. It was actually a good thing that Mallory hadn't gone to the police or Crane might have tried to silence her, too, the way he'd gone after Alyssa. "Do you remember anything else?"

"No. I wish I did. I wish I had proof I could simply hand over to you." She looked totally dejected. He found himself wanting to reassure her, to make her feel better.

Which was totally ridiculous.

Getting too close to someone in the case was unacceptable. Hadn't he learned that the hard way? It only took a fraction of a second to bring the image of his partner's widow to mind.

He'd failed his partner, Drew Massey, when he'd lowered his guard with a young drug runner. And when Drew's wife, Elaine, had accused him of causing

Drew's death, he couldn't defend himself. Because she'd been right. Thanks to the eyewitness's cell-phone video, the whole world had been able to see how he'd failed his partner. Including his fiancée. Cheryl had wasted no time in leaving him.

"I'm sorry, Jonah," she said, interrupting his tumultuous thoughts. "I wish now that I had paid more attention."

"Don't worry about it. Why don't you try to get some sleep? I'm not planning to stop for a while yet."

"I'll try," she murmured.

She didn't sleep, but she didn't talk, either. He was oddly relieved to discover Mallory wasn't the type to fill a silence with small talk.

No matter how much he told himself to keep an open mind, deep down, he believed Mallory's story. For the past twenty-four hours, he'd been hoping that finding her would be the key to blowing his case wide open. But overhearing a snippet of a conversation wouldn't get him anywhere close to pressing charges. If they couldn't corroborate Mallory's story, they had nothing.

Which meant not only was Mallory's life still in danger, but he was right back to square one.

Mallory yawned so wide her jaw popped. She scrubbed at her gritty eyes, trying to force herself to stay awake. Finally, just as dawn was breaking over the horizon, Jonah pulled into a motel with a flashing vacancy sign out front.

"Where are we?" she asked, realizing she hadn't even noticed the name of the town.

"Glen Hollow," Jonah replied as he shut off the car and opened his door. "Population less than nine hundred."

She slid out of the passenger seat. "Honestly, as long as there's running water and a shower, I don't care how many people live here."

He flashed a tired grin, and she was struck by how handsome Jonah was. He wasn't overly tall, just barely six feet in her estimation, but he was muscular. And she liked the way he wore his dark hair short. He opened the back door and rummaged around in a duffel bag. Before she could ask what he was doing, he stripped off his old shirt, revealing the blood-stained dressing covering the right side of his chest, before he pulled a black T-shirt over his head.

She turned away, feeling light-headed but unsure whether it was the blood or Jonah causing the sensation.

Must be the blood because she was immune to handsome men. She only dated men on her terms, determined to be the one in control. Never again would she let her guard down.

"Wait for me in the car," he said in a low voice. "I don't want the clerk to be able to identify you."

Unable to argue with his logic, she

nodded and slid back into the passenger seat. It was only a few minutes before he returned.

"Here." He handed her a key. "We have adjoining rooms, numbers ten and twelve."

"Ah, okay." She was surprised he cared enough to respect her need for privacy. She couldn't remember the last guy who'd put her needs before his own.

She told herself not to place too much emphasis on Jonah's kindness. For all she knew, he was simply biding his time before he slipped handcuffs on her and hauled her off to jail.

If he tried that, he'd learn firsthand what it meant to be a black belt in Tae Kwon Do.

Jonah grabbed his laptop and his duffel bag from the backseat of his car. He caught Mallory eyeing his duffel with longing. Luckily he had plenty of cash—

there would be time to pick up a few things for her later.

They went into their rooms. Jonah dropped his duffel bag on the bed and then crossed over to unlock the connecting door on his side of the two rooms. He was surprised to find that Mallory had already opened her side, too. He hovered in the doorway, not wanting to encroach on her personal space. The faint scent of juniper greeted him, as if Mallory had stashed a few Christmas trees inside. "I—uh—thought we'd head over to the diner for breakfast before we get some sleep."

"Sure." Her smile was weary. "But if you could stop at the front desk to get me a toothbrush, I'd appreciate it."

"No problem." He grabbed his computer and followed her outside.

She glanced at the computer in surprise. "Do you really think the café has Wi-Fi?"

"According to the desk clerk they do."

He'd made sure there was an internet connection in the rooms, too. "Figured I'd do some research on your former boyfriend over breakfast."

Mallory didn't say anything in response, but followed him inside the café. He chose a booth in the back. But when he booted up the computer, Mallory slid in beside him.

"What are you doing?" he asked in alarm, trying to ignore her juniper scent.

"I'm not just going to sit there and watch you work," Mallory said in exasperation. "I can help."

He wished he'd brought more than one computer, to keep Mallory on the opposite side of the booth where she belonged. Yet he could hardly blame her for wanting to help. When the waitress came over with a pot of coffee, he stopped her from filling his cup. "Just orange juice for me, please."

"Me, too," Mallory chimed in.

While they waited for their order, he

began to search for recent information about Anthony Caruso.

"Do you know what we're looking for?" Mallory asked.

"A needle in a haystack," he muttered. His computer skills were decent, but attempting to breach the security of a state senator's home computer probably wasn't smart, especially on a public network, so he refrained. Thinking clearly wasn't easy with Mallory glued to his side. He hadn't been this distracted by a woman in a long time.

And he shouldn't be now, while he was in the middle of a case.

They took a break from the computer search when their food arrived, and thankfully Mallory went back to her side of the booth. Neither of them said much as they ate. His original plan was to stay at the café and work while Mallory went back to the room to get some sleep. But exhaustion was already weighing him down.

Once they'd finished breakfast, Mallory again abandoned her side of the booth to slide in beside him.

"Why don't you cross-reference Caruso's name with Jefferson's?" she suggested.

He typed in the two names, and the first item to come up was a newspaper article regarding a charity event that had been held a week ago, down at the Pfister Hotel in Milwaukee. When a color photo bloomed on the screen, he heard Mallory gasp softly.

"What's wrong?" he asked. And then he noticed the slender woman in a deep blue gown standing off to the side. The photographer had only caught her back, but the woman's short, curly blond hair matched Mallory's. He glanced over at her as he lightly tapped the computer screen. "This is you, isn't it?"

"Yes. I attended the event with Anthony—he's in the photo, too, right here, but you can't see him very well." Her face had gone pale as she stared at the photo.

"Did you remember something from that night?" he pressed, watching her carefully. "Maybe another conversation you overheard?"

"Anthony was angry when this guy came by to take our pictures. In fact, at the time I thought he was completely overreacting when he had stomped over to the photographer, demanding the photo be erased from his digital camera. Of course the camera guy had refused, and Hugh Jefferson had come over to calm down Anthony. Anthony and Jefferson went off to talk, and the next thing I knew, the entire incident was glossed over. When I asked Anthony about it later, he told me not to worry about it, because Jefferson convinced the cameraman not to list his name."

He frowned and glanced back at the photograph he'd enlarged on the screen. "Strikes me as odd that the senator didn't want his picture taken. Normally politicians love to be splashed all over the media."

She nodded slowly. "Yeah, I thought it was odd, too. In fact, up until that point, I hadn't heard Anthony raise his voice to anyone. I think that was partially why I listened to his phone conversation the next night. He was always so smoothly charming."

He swiveled in his seat to stare at her. "Are you telling me this charity event was the night before you overheard him trying to cover up Councilman Schaefer's murder?"

"Yes. The benefit was on Thursday night, and I overheard the conversation the next day. We'd originally made plans to have lunch, but then Anthony backed out, saying something important at work had come up. Next thing I knew, he was talking about covering up a murder."

His gut clenched when he realized how lucky she'd been to get away from

Caruso's thug not just once, but twice. He was thankful Mallory had managed to get away, or the outcome of Wasserman's attack could have been very different.

God was definitely watching over her. Watching over both of them.

And this time, he wouldn't mess up like he had the night his partner had died.

Please, God, give me the strength and the knowledge to keep Mallory safe.

He stared at the surprisingly clear photograph. It was easy to recognize Senator Caruso now that she'd pointed him out. But why would the guy go to a public charity event only to become upset when he was photographed? None of this made any sense.

Had something else happened that night? Something significant enough to put Caruso on edge? Something that may have sent the entire house of cards that Jefferson built tumbling to the ground?

His blood ran cold.

What if Mallory had become a target not just because she'd overheard Caruso's patio conversation, but because she saw or heard something with even more significance? Something so damaging, Caruso had no choice but to silence her forever?

THREE

Mallory rubbed the back of her neck. Holding her head at an awkward angle in order to read Jonah's computer screen was giving her a neck ache to match her headache.

They were crazy to think they might find something on the internet that would lead them to incriminating evidence against Anthony Caruso. She eased away from Jonah and reached for her orange juice.

She was too exhausted to do any more surfing and Jonah must have been, too, since he shut down the computer and pulled out his wallet to pay the bill.

"I have some cash, too, if you need some," she offered.

He scowled, apparently chauvinistic enough to dislike the idea of a woman paying her own way. "I'm fine. Let's go. We both need a couple hours of sleep."

She followed him out of the café and across the street to their motel rooms. He opened the door, checking to make sure the room was safe before he stood back and allowed her to go inside.

"Keep the connecting door unlocked, okay? Just in case."

Just in case what? She suppressed a shiver. "There's no way the ski-mask guy could have followed us, right?"

"No. But we can't afford to let down our guard, either. Just humor me, okay?"

She hesitated and then nodded. "Okay."

Jonah stared at her for a moment, as if he wanted to say more, but then he turned and disappeared inside his room. She partially closed the connecting door on her side, before testing out the running water in the bathroom—which was pure bliss—and then climbing into bed. She fell asleep the instant her head hit the pillow.

Mallory had no idea how long she slept, but much like the night before, a strange sound dragged her awake. She stayed perfectly still, straining to listen.

She heard it again. A muffled sound coming from Jonah's room. She climbed from her bed, pulled on her grungy clothes and pushed open the connecting door.

Jonah was talking in his sleep, thrashing on the bed, obviously in the throes of a nightmare. She crossed over to shake his shoulder. "Jonah, wake up. You're having a bad dream."

Almost instantly, he shot upward and grabbed his gun. She shrank away, holding out her hand to calm him down. "It's me, Jonah. Mallory. I was only trying to wake you up from your nightmare."

He slowly lowered his weapon, letting out his breath in a heavy sigh. "I'm sorry. I— You took me by surprise."

He avoided her gaze. A faint sheen of sweat covered his face and dampened the hair at his temples. Definitely a nightmare. "Jonah, who's Drew? You were muttering something about Drew."

His expression closed, and she sensed that whatever the source of his nightmare, he wasn't inclined to talk about it. "I'm sorry I woke you."

"No need to apologize." She noticed with surprise that the Gideon Bible was lying open on his bedside table. Had Jonah actually been reading the Bible? The only person she knew who'd ever read the Bible on a regular basis was Alyssa.

He must have noticed her gaze because he flashed a lopsided smile. "Renewing my faith helps me relax, especially in times of stress. You might want to give it a try."

She frowned and shook her head. "No

thanks. Not after everything I've been through."

He frowned, but didn't look surprised by her attitude. "I'm sure you have your reasons for not believing, Mallory, but have you ever considered how God might help shoulder your burden rather than add to it?"

She wished there was a tactful way to change the subject. "You have no idea what I've been through. Having Anthony Caruso attempt to kill me isn't the worst I've suffered." She told herself to shut up before she found herself blubbering about her past.

The last thing she wanted or needed was Jonah's sympathy.

"You're right, Mallory. I don't know everything you've suffered. But I do know about my own experience." There was a long pause before he continued. "Drew was my partner. He was a few years older than me, and he taught me everything I needed to know about being a cop."

The stark agony in his eyes made her wish she'd never asked about his nightmare. She knew, only too well, how reliving the past only made it harder to forget.

"One day, we caught this kid running drugs. He was young, barely eleven, and I wanted the guy who was pulling the strings on this kid. Drew wanted to haul him in, but I convinced him to try it my way first. The kid was so young, and he looked up at me with big eyes, telling me he'd show us where he was supposed to take the money. I believed him. Drew tried to talk me out of it, but I insisted. The kid led us right into a trap."

She gasped, the scene so vivid she felt as if she was right there with him.

"And when the shooting started, I instinctively protected the kid who'd betrayed us, leaving my partner open. He died as a result of my actions." Jonah's expression was grim as he faced her. "So while I don't know what you've been through, Mallory, I do know that God can help carry a heavy burden."

A long silence stretched between them, and she had no idea what to say. But she realized that Jonah's past was just as difficult to live with as hers.

Jonah reached out to touch the Bible. "Without faith, I would never have made it through the worst time of my life."

She gave a helpless shrug. "I guess I just don't understand how believing in God helps."

"It's hard to explain," he admitted. "But I can tell you that God doesn't abandon us when we need Him. He's there for us, always."

She didn't believe God was there for her. Not back when she was seventeen, or when Caruso's thug tried to kill her.

Unless God had sent Jonah to save her?

No, she didn't really believe that, and

this wasn't the time or place to argue with Jonah over religion.

"Maybe at some point, you'll give it a try," Jonah said. "However, right now, we need to think of some way to get evidence against Caruso."

She was glad he let the subject drop. "I went back over the night of the fundraiser, and there is one other thing I remember. Although I'm not sure it means much."

He leaned forward. "What is it?"

"There was a brief disagreement between Jefferson and Caruso. I didn't really pay much attention then, but looking back, it was right about the time Jefferson took a phone call. I think the news may have been about Schaefer."

"Can you remember exactly what was said? By either Jefferson or Caruso?"

"Caruso said something like, 'I wouldn't have to worry if you weren't such an amateur.'" She wished she'd heard what they were saying. "At the time, I assumed they were talking about investments, but now I'm thinking the conversation may have referred to having Schaefer stabbed and being forced to attribute the stabbing to gang activity."

"You could be right. Nice detective work, Mallory."

She blushed and shrugged off the compliment. No doubt Jonah was simply trying to stay on her good side. "So now what? Where do we go from here?"

He scrubbed his hands over his face. "Good question. Give me some time to pull myself together, and I'll try to come up with a plan."

"As long as your plan doesn't involve me turning myself in to the D.A.," she murmured as she turned away. No matter how good of a detective Jonah was, he couldn't possibly find proof she couldn't even be sure existed. And they couldn't stay on the run forever—they both had jobs, careers to get back to.

A wave of hopelessness washed over

her. For a fleeting moment, she surprised herself and considered trying to pray. Except she didn't know how and didn't really think God would listen to someone like her even if she did.

She was better off relying only on herself—the way she'd always done.

Jonah examined his incision as well as he could in the mirror above the sink in the bathroom. It looked worse than he'd anticipated. He applied some antibacterial ointment before slapping a new gauze dressing over the area where he'd popped two stitches. At least the wound had stopped bleeding. He was glad Alyssa had forced him to bring first-aid supplies, although she'd no doubt be upset that he'd opened the wound. Belatedly remembering his antibiotics, he popped one, hoping the pills would be strong enough to ward off infection.

For a moment he stared grimly at his reflection in the mirror. What he really needed to do was call his boss and ask for someone else to watch over Mallory. Not only was he still recuperating from his stab wound and subsequent surgery, he also was too close to making the same mistake he had in the past—letting his emotions get in the way of his job.

He couldn't cross the line and begin caring about Mallory. He never should have accepted her help in finding evidence against Caruso. She wasn't a cop. What he needed to do was to convince his boss to put her up in some sort of safe house. A place where able-bodied cops could watch over her instead of a wounded warrior like him.

As he dressed, his cell phone rang. He picked up his phone to see who'd called.

He was expecting his boss, but it was Gage. Knowing Mallory would be thrilled to hear from her sister, he crossed over to gently tap on the door between their rooms. "Mallory? It's Gage. Do you want to talk?"

"Yes!" She eagerly took the phone. "Alyssa?" Her face lit up with joy, and he turned away to give her some privacy. "What happened?"

Jonah knew Alyssa would fill Mallory in on everything, in much greater detail than he had. He went back into his room and waited. When she was done, he'd call his boss.

Mallory didn't return for a good fifteen minutes, but when she handed him the phone, she was smiling. "Alyssa's fine. She told me everything and then offered to blow off her surgery to come up here. I convinced her to stay put and take care of herself. Thankfully, for the first time ever, Gage agreed with me."

"I'm glad." He took the phone and punched in his boss's number.

"Who are you calling?" she asked.

"My boss. Lieutenant Michael Finley."

Her jaw dropped open in shock. "Your boss? I thought you said Alyssa sent you. I didn't realize you were reporting everything to your boss." She'd trusted Jonah with her life and didn't appreciate how he'd held back important information.

"I'm keeping Finley updated. He knows the plan is to find the top guy involved in Jefferson's money- laundering scheme. Jefferson used way too much cash, and we were also able to trace his funds for the condo project to a Swiss bank account. I need to let Finley know we suspect Caruso."

The expression on her face indicated she wasn't happy with that news. "I thought you said there was a warrant out for my arrest."

"There is, but I think I can convince Finley you're being framed for Wasserman's murder. And I think he'll agree to put you up in a safe house."

"A safe house?" She glared at him with dismay. "Why would I want to do that? I'd rather stay with you."

He hardened his heart against the hurt

reflected in her eyes. But he refused to let his emotions sway his decision. Putting Mallory in a safe house was the right thing to do. "Because you need to be safe, no matter what."

"Oh, yeah?" Her blue eyes narrowed with suspicion. "And what about you?"

He looked away. "Once I know you're safe, I plan to head back to Milwaukee or maybe even Chicago so I can find hard evidence against Caruso."

Mallory watched with helpless anger as Jonah went outside to make his phone call, obviously seeking privacy. She went over to the door but she was unable to decipher any specific words. Dejected, she went back to her own room, waiting in the connecting doorway for him to return.

What had she done to make Jonah so anxious to be rid of her? Apparently the closeness she believed might be growing between them was nothing more than her overactive imagination. No big surprise there. She couldn't help feeling hurt by the idea he'd leave her alone in a police safe house while continuing his investigation without her.

Apparently, Jonah preferred to work alone.

Granted, she didn't exactly have the skills or background that Jonah did, but she knew Anthony Caruso on a personal level. Certainly that knowledge alone gave her some value.

When Jonah returned to the motel room, his closed expression reinforced her deepest fears. She wanted to scream and yell that he couldn't leave her alone in some safe house, but knew instinctively that theatrics weren't going to sway him off course.

Through the open connecting doors between their rooms, she saw that he'd picked up the Bible. The way he settled down to read, as if he didn't have a care in the world, made her seethe with frustration. What was wrong with him? Didn't he have any feelings for her at all?

Of course he didn't, she reminded herself sternly. She wasn't the type of woman he could ever care about on a personal level. She didn't believe in God the way he did, for one thing. And she was part of his case against Caruso. A woman he was responsible for protecting. Until he could hand her over to someone else.

"Mallory? Are you all right?"

His soft question pulled her from her thoughts. "No, I'm not. But why would you bother asking? Haven't you already decided the next step without caring about what I want?"

When he glanced away, she knew her point had hit home. Being right didn't make her feel any better, though.

Jonah was silent for several long minutes. "'He will cover you with his feathers, and under his wings you will find refuge; his faithfulness will be your shield and rampart,'" Jonah murmured.

The phrase didn't sound the least bit familiar, but struck a chord deep within, nonetheless. "Is that really from the Bible? It sounds more like a poem." She was intrigued by the lyrical words.

"In a way. The Book of Psalms reads like a book of poems."

She was surprised to hear Bible verses actually read like poems. She'd always thought they were dry and preachy. Alyssa's friends had been involved in church activities, but she'd resisted going along, no matter how much Alyssa tried to convince her. Reluctantly curious, she walked across the threshold into his room to see for herself. As she approached, she caught sight of Jonah's car keys sitting on top of the dresser. Without giving herself time to consider the consequences of her actions, she silently swept them into her hand and stuck them into the front pocket of her sweatshirt.

"Here, start at the beginning," Jonah urged.

She took the Bible from his hands and tried to read but she couldn't concentrate. The car keys were practically burning a hole clear through the fleece to her skin. Finally, she handed the Bible back to Jonah. "Sorry, it doesn't really work for me."

The flash of disappointment in his eyes shouldn't have bothered her. She turned and tried not to rush as she made her way back to her room.

Once she was out of his line of vision, she paused long enough to take a deep breath. She looped her purse over her shoulder and tried to edge closer to the door.

She felt bad about leaving him here, but he'd called his boss, hadn't he? Someone would be here soon enough to rescue him. By that time she'd be far out of reach.

She didn't know how to explain to Jonah why she didn't trust anyone but him. Partially because Gage and Alyssa had vouched for his integrity. Partially because he believed in God.

And most of all, because she liked him. She couldn't remember the last time she had met a man she actually liked. A man she felt comfortable being around. She didn't need to constantly have her guard up with Jonah.

She crossed to the door and silently turned the handle. Holding her breath, she opened it, slipped through and tried to shut it quietly behind her.

But she'd only gone two steps when Jonah's door burst open. She was shocked speechless when he grabbed her hand, prying the car keys from her numb fingers. It happened so fast, she didn't have a chance to react, to strike out with a roundhouse kick or a blow to his arm.

Or maybe she just couldn't bring herself to hit Jonah.

"Nice try, Mallory," he said in a patronizing tone.

A red haze of fury blinded her. "Let me go! I'd rather be out there on my own than stuck in some safe house with someone I don't know!"

"Why?" he demanded, sliding the car keys deep into his pocket, far out of her reach. "I'm only doing this for your own good, Mallory. Can't you understand I want you to be safe?"

She ground her teeth together, fighting the urge to pummel him with her fists. Were all men this annoying? She'd never been emotionally involved enough to find out. "You said yourself that there was a dirty cop working with Jefferson, helping him from the inside. How do you know there aren't more? How do you know that Officer Crane, the cop who died, wasn't working with someone?"

He stood there, staring at her uncertainly. Sensing she might have an edge, she pushed a little more.

"Jonah, think about it. Can you live with your decision, knowing there is a slim chance Caruso might find me and kill me inside the safe house?" She held her breath, hoping, praying he'd understand.

Because the last thing she wanted to do was go off on her own——without Jonah Stewart.

FOUR

Jonah closed his fist around the car keys in his hand, barely feeling the hard metal edges cutting into his flesh. He'd been shocked to notice his keys were gone and had luckily caught Mallory before she could get away. As mad as he was, he couldn't blame her for trying to leave, any more than he could deny the truth underscoring Mallory's words.

But no matter how tempted he might be to sympathize with her, he couldn't allow himself to be swayed off course.

He couldn't live with himself if he failed Mallory. Logically, he knew stashing her in a safe house was his best option. A cop who wasn't recovering from a stab wound and surgery would be able to protect her better than he could. Whether she believed it or not.

"I'm sorry, Mallory. But the best course of action for me is to return to Milwaukee, and likely to Chicago, in order to find evidence against Caruso."

"Take me with you," she begged.

Feeling his resolve soften, he dragged his gaze away from hers. "I can't. You'll only slow me down. Besides, I need to know you're safe."

"And what if I'm not safe?" she challenged. "What if there's another dirty cop who finds a way to get to me?"

He couldn't bear to think of Mallory being in danger. But he also didn't think Aaron Crane had been working with another cop on the inside. From what little information he and his boss could piece together, they believed Crane had been working alone. "Lieutenant Finley assured me he'll find two men he can trust to stay with you at the safe house. I've been communicating with him since this mess started and I have no reason to believe he won't hold up his end of the deal."

She stared at him, stark resignation in her gaze. "Well, then, I guess there's nothing more to discuss." Her voice simmered with betrayal. She turned her back on him and returned to her room, closing the door behind her softly. Why he would have felt better if she'd slammed it, he had no idea.

For a moment he stared and then slowly made his way back inside, not at all surprised to discover Mallory had closed the connecting door.

Reminding himself he'd made this decision for her own good didn't make him feel any better. When his cell phone rang, he was thankful for the diversion from his thoughts. "Hey, Gage, what's up?"

"Not much, other than Alyssa is officially scheduled for surgery. They're going to operate first thing in the morning."

"Wow, that's fast."

"Yeah, although not as far as Alyssa's concerned. She's anxious for it to be done and over."

"I don't blame her. And I'm glad she and Mallory had time to talk." He was glad Mallory had already spoken to her sister, because he knew Alyssa would side with Mallory if the two of them talked now.

"Hey, when Mallory told Alyssa about Anthony Caruso, I did a little digging and stumbled across some information."

"Mallory told Alyssa about Caruso?" For some reason, that surprised him.

"Yeah, Alyssa was mad at herself for not recognizing him earlier, when she found a photo of the two of them together in Mallory's dresser."

He scowled, not exactly thrilled to hear Mallory had hidden a photo of Caruso in her condo. Was she upset about their broken relationship? He didn't sense she was grieving over it, but then again, he had the impression that Mallory was good at hiding her feelings. "Don't keep me in suspense, Gage. What did you find out?"

"I looked into who exactly supported Caruso's political career. Not surprisingly, Hugh Jefferson was on the list along with Eric Holden."

"You're right, that's not surprising." Too bad they hadn't stumbled across that connection much sooner, since Holden, a newly elected Milwaukee mayor, financially supporting Caruso, a U.S. state senator from Illinois, might have raised a red flag. Local politics were one thing, but why support someone in a different state? Unless you just happened to be in business together.

"The name that jumped out at me was Bernardo Salvatore, who owns a handful of Sicilian restaurants across the Midwest. From what I found online, he was planning to open a brand-new restaurant in downtown Milwaukee, less than a mile from Jefferson's condo project. However, now the plans are on hold, indefinitely."

Jonah could hardly suppress the buzz of excitement from the slim lead. The connection was worth investigating. "So Bernardo Salvatore is in league with Caruso."

"Possibly," Gage admitted. "At least it's something to work on. I wanted to let you know so you could start down that path, since Jefferson, Holden and Crane are all dead."

"Not your fault, Gage." Jonah knew his buddy was still blaming himself for allowing Alyssa to be caught and for inadvertently causing the fire on the yacht, which killed both Holden and Jefferson before they could get any information out of them. "We'll get Caruso, sooner or later. Maybe he'll make another mistake. If he thinks Mallory is the only threat at this point, he might be running his money-laundering scheme in a business-as-usual mode."

"I hope so. Jonah, be careful, okay?" Gage's concerned tone wasn't exactly reassuring. "One more death isn't going to weigh too heavily on Caruso's conscience. In fact, if Caruso somehow discovers you're involved with helping Mallory, you'll be marked as a threat he'll need to eliminate, right along with her."

"Won't be the first time some crook wants me dead," he said, downplaying his friend's concern. "Talk to you later."

"Yeah, later."

Jonah stared out the window, grimly realizing he'd made a mistake last night by allowing the ski-masked intruder to get away. Whoever Caruso hired to take out Mallory now knew she wasn't alone.

He fully believed that dirty cop, Aaron Crane, had attacked him on Jefferson's orders. And since Jefferson reported up to Caruso, he figured Caruso knew he'd escaped. How long before Caruso realized that he was the one who helped Mallory escape?

Several hours later, Jonah walked across the street to the gas station minimart to pick up additional medical supplies for his wound that wouldn't stop bleeding, along with a couple sandwiches and some chips. He'd decided against returning to the café, just on the off chance that someone had stopped by to ask about them.

There was a black Lab tied up outside but the dog didn't seem overly anxious about a stranger going inside. Apparently, the gas station was the main source of income for the town and the dog was accustomed to strangers.

After returning to the motel, he knocked on the connecting door between their rooms, hoping Mallory would accept his offer of peace.

A long minute passed, making Jonah wonder if she'd decided to ignore him, but then she opened the door, the expression on her face less than welcoming. "Has your replacement arrived yet?"

"Not yet." He lifted the bag. "I brought lunch."

She eyed the bag curiously, and eventually hunger won out over anger. She stepped back and allowed him to come in. He saw an open Bible on the bed, and he couldn't help crossing over to see what had captured her interest. "Are you reading the Book of Psalms?" he asked in surprise.

She lifted a shoulder in a shrug and color rose to her cheeks as if she were embarrassed. "They make more sense when you start at the beginning."

Humbled and pleased, he realized that he might be helping her discover her faith. Of course, just reading the Book of Psalms didn't mean she would become a believer, but he couldn't help thinking he might be able to help sway her opinion if they had time to talk. Maybe attend church. Did the town have a church?

Maybe he shouldn't have called his boss for assistance so quickly. Was it possible God placed Mallory in his path not only to keep her safe from physical harm, but to assist her in finding her way to God?

If so, he was eager to accept God's calling. He closed his eyes and prayed for strength. Mallory watched him intently, but before he could pursue the issue, she changed the subject.

"Would you mind if I borrow your phone after we're finished eating? I'd like to find out how Alyssa is doing. She mentioned she had an MRI done of her ankle."

"Sure. In fact, I spoke to Gage earlier and he said everything went well." When he saw the annoyance flash in her eyes at being left out of the conversation, he quickly added, "Alyssa is scheduled for surgery first thing tomorrow morning. If you want to talk to her again, I'm sure Gage wouldn't mind."

"I guess there's no rush." Looking slightly mollified, she took another bite of her sandwich. "Jonah, would you consider sending me to stay with Alyssa and Gage instead? At least then I wouldn't be at the mercy of strangers."

He thought her statement was odd. Why would she feel she was at the mercy of strangers? Did she really think two cops posed some sort of threat?

"Mallory, if you go home, you'll be putting both Gage and Alyssa at risk. Especially Alyssa, who will obviously be unable to move very well after undergoing surgery." He'd left the hospital against medical advice right after the surgery to repair his deflated lung, and those first few days had been awful. Of course, running around the city chasing Jefferson hadn't exactly helped his recuperation.

"Okay, but couldn't they come to the safe house with me?" she persisted. "If this place is as safe as you think, they wouldn't be in danger."

He couldn't argue her point. And it was possible Gage could be persuaded to go along with her plan, if only to appease Alyssa. "We'll discuss the possibility with Gage, okay? If he agrees, then I'm happy to make the arrangements, once she's home from surgery."

"Great. Thanks, Jonah." Mallory's mood lightened considerably, and he couldn't help wondering what had happened in her past to make trust so difficult. "Do you mind if I ask you another question?" she asked.

He dragged his thoughts to the present. "Of course not."

"Do you really believe God forgives all sins?"

"Absolutely." Now he knew God really had sent him to assist Mallory in finding her way home. Her question touched him. "'Through Jesus the forgiveness of sins is proclaimed to you,'" he quoted.

She was silent for a long moment. "Even if the sins are really bad?" she asked in a voice so soft, he had to lean closer to hear.

"Yes, even if the sins are really bad. It's never too late to turn your life around, Mallory, never too late to accept God and your faith. But I find it hard to believe your sins are as bad as you claim."

She frowned. "You don't know enough about me to say that, Jonah." Avoiding his gaze, she leaped up from the table and began clearing away the mess from their meal. "I'd like to call Gage now, if you don't mind."

He silently handed her his cell phone. Feeling restless, he crossed over to his own room, standing next to the window and staring at the highway leading into town. A few dark clouds dotted the sky, but nothing too serious. He was surprised his replacements hadn't arrived yet.

Just ten minutes later, Mallory returned his phone. "Your boss called," she said.

"Did you get to talk to Alyssa?"

"Yes." Mallory flashed a brief smile. "She's a little worried about the surgery, but is thankful Gage will be there for her. I'm thrilled she's giving Gage a second chance."

"They're good together." He called Finley back, prepared for bad news. "Hi, boss, what's up?"

"I won't be able to free anyone up to relieve you until tomorrow. Stay right where you are, and I promise I'll have someone there first thing in the morning."

He sighed and rubbed the back of his neck. It was late afternoon, nearly four o'clock. "Okay, I suppose another sixteen hours won't make much of a difference."

"If anything changes, I'll let you know."

Jonah ended the call and crossed over to the connecting door between their rooms. "Make yourself comfortable. We're staying here for another night."

She didn't look overly disappointed. "Another night is fine with me. Maybe we could go to the hospital tomorrow to visit Alyssa?"

"Mallory, you know we can't take that risk." He didn't have the heart to remind her that Gage hadn't agreed to their plan yet, either. And even if Gage did agree, Alyssa wouldn't be ready for a few days. Better to give Mallory something positive to look forward to.

Now that he had extra time on his hands, he decided to keep digging into Caruso's and Salvatore's business holdings. There had to be another connection, besides just campaign support.

He worked on his computer for several hours, until the stupid thing died. With a scowl, he looked to make sure the power cord was plugged in. Was the outlet broken? The computer battery had gone dead, indicating the power had been off for a while, so he tried several outlets around the room, without success.

Was there something wrong with the power? He crossed the room, intending to flip on the switch to test his theory, but just then the black Lab outside the gas station began to bark.

Jonah crossed over to the window. The sun was low on the horizon, but there was still plenty of light to see. He could easily make out the image of the large black dog straining against the confines of his leash, staring in the direction of the motel.

The hair on the back of Jonah's neck rose in warning. Something was wrong. Very wrong. And then he noticed an orange glow reflected in the window of the gas station.

Their motel was on fire.

Grabbing the car keys off the dresser, he threw open the door between their rooms. "Mallory?" He crossed over to shake her awake. "Hurry, we need to get out of here right now."

To her credit, she didn't argue. She rose up off the bed, pushing her hair out of her eyes as she reached for her purse. "Why? What's going on?"

"The motel is on fire." He tried to open her door but it didn't budge. Panic surged as he tried the door again, putting more muscle into it.

Still, the door didn't give. He ran over to check his door, with the same results.

The fire was no accident. They were locked in.

Mallory's nerves were already on edge from the incessant barking of the dog, but when she realized they were trapped, her pulse soared. Illogically, she tried the door herself, as if she would be able to open the door that Jonah couldn't.

The distinct smell of smoke made her wrinkle her nose in distaste. "I don't understand. I didn't hear any thunder. Could lightning have struck the building?"

"No." He came out of the bathroom, two soaking-wet towels in his hand and another towel wrapped around his fist. "Take these and hold them over your face." He tossed the wet towels in her direction. "Stand back."

Before she could ask him anything more, there was a loud crash as he punched out the window. The dog continued to bark and she realized the black Lab may have saved their lives. Jonah swept the shards of glass out of the way, and for the second time in only three nights, he helped her escape.

Outside, the heat from the fire was intense. Glancing over her shoulder, she realized the entire second floor was burning. There wasn't a storm. In fact, there weren't even very many clouds in the sky. There was a loud crack and Jonah grabbed her arm, pulling her out of the way as the roof collapsed.

"Run," he urged, pulling her in the opposite direction from where their rental car was parked.

"The rental car is back that way," she argued, digging in her heels. Surely he didn't intend for them to leave this miniscule town on foot?

"Forget about the car," he said, dragging her along against her will. "We're going this way."

Jonah pulled her toward a cornfield. She tried not to think about the horror movie involving a cornfield she'd watched as a kid, as she followed him down between the rows.

"Try to be quiet," he whispered.

She couldn't help glancing back over her shoulder, gasping at how the orange glow from the fire lit up the sky. She shivered, in spite of the chill in the air. With the tall green stalks of corn surrounding them, her fear of tight places became overwhelming. "Jonah," she warned.

"What?"

"We have to get out of here—I'm claustrophobic." She struggled to control her breathing, but it wasn't easy. She was unable to ignore the corn husks surrounding them—they kept slapping at her arms, legs and face. Only bugs would have been worse. Spiders. Instantly her skin crawled with imaginary insects and she rubbed her hands vigorously over her arms.

"Hang on, Mallory, for just a little while longer."

She wasn't sure she could hang on. How could Jonah see where they were going? What if they got lost in the cornfields? She'd never survive if they had to spend the night here. Panic swelled. Maybe it was because she'd read the Bible earlier, but a prayer popped into her mind.

Please, Lord, guide us to safety.

Surprisingly, she felt calmer after her murmured prayer. She took a couple deep breaths and glanced up at the sky, hoping the sun wouldn't slip behind the horizon just yet. Seeing the open space overhead helped.

Jonah kept moving and, thankfully, seemed to know exactly where he was going. A good fifteen minutes later, they burst out of the cornfield.

Thank You, Lord, she whispered, stopping long enough to catch her breath.

Jonah stood close beside her, keeping a hand on her arm as if he were afraid he'd lose her. "Ready?" he asked.

"For what?" She glanced around, trying to figure out which direction the highway might be. "It's going to be dark soon, and we won't be able to find our way."

"We only have to go a little farther, Mallory," Jonah urged. "But we need to hurry."

She thought it was possible he was losing his mind, but since following him was better than standing in the middle of a field, she decided to go along.

There was a humming sound that seemed to gradually grow louder. "Come on, Mallory. Hurry."

Hurry? What on earth did he mean? It wasn't until she saw the train tracks that she understood what the sound was. "Is that a train?"

"Cargo train. I saw it go by earlier today." Jonah walked over to the edge of the train tracks and turned until he faced south.

The sound of the train engine grew louder, and suddenly she knew what Jonah intended. "No, I can't," she said with a horrified gasp.

"You have to," he insisted, his hand tightening around hers. "Mallory, if you want to get out of this place, we have to jump aboard the train."

She felt as if she were frozen in place

as the light of the train approached. The train was going too fast. Jonah was nuts if he thought they could really do this.

"Ready?" he asked, running alongside the train.

"No!" she shouted, the sound of her voice drowned out by the train as it went by.

"Now, Mallory!" he yelled directly into her ear. "Grab one of those railings! I'll be right behind you!"

Her heart lodged in her throat as she ran. She gauged the distance to the railing the way she would if she were about to do a jumping snap kick to break boards in Tae Kwon Do.

She took a deep breath, jumped and grabbed. She cried out in surprise as pain shot up her arm from being wrenched off her feet. Ignoring the pain, she found another handhold along the edge of the car, securing her precarious position.

She'd made it! She wanted to laugh and cry at the same time.

Feeling like Spider-Man clinging to the side of a building, she lifted her head and glanced to her left, peering intently through the darkness.

She'd made it safely on the train—but where was Jonah?

FIVE

Mallory tried to rein in her panic, taking several deep breaths. What if Jonah hadn't made it on the train? She wanted to believe he was farther back because he'd forced her to go first, but what if he had misjudged the distance and hadn't made it at all?

She was too afraid to move, even though she knew she couldn't just stay here like this forever. Would the train slow down at some point? Or did it keep going at the same speed until they reached their destination? And how many miles away was their destination anyway?

"Mallory!" Jonah's voice brought a rush of relief. She looked to the right and could have kissed him when she saw him standing in the opening, on a narrow metal ledge between the two cars. "Grab my hand."

She stared in terror as Jonah reached out for her. The thought of letting go of the metal railing only made her tighten her grip. "I can't."

"Sure you can. The distance is only about a foot. Let go of the railing with your right hand and reach out for me. I'll do the rest."

She looked at him across the distance, trying to trust him. Her eyes pricked with tears, but she told herself they were only watering from the force of the wind whipping past. Tightening her grip with her left hand, she took a deep breath and let go of the railing. When Jonah's fingers closed strongly around hers, she let out a gasp of relief.

True to his word, the rest was easy. With Jonah's guidance, she managed to find firmer footing on the small platform between the two cars. When his arms closed around her, she leaned against him, burying her face against his chest.

"It's okay," Jonah said, speaking close to her ear so she could hear as he rubbed a soothing hand over her back. "You were very brave, Mallory. We're safe now."

She wished she could believe the part about being safe. As far as she could tell, they'd have to keep running forever. She lifted her head to look up at him.

"What happened back at the motel, Jonah?" She had to speak loudly so he could hear over the noise of the train. "How could Caruso's thug have found us so quickly? Do you think he followed your car?"

Jonah's gaze darkened with anger. "I suppose he might have gotten the license plate number, but I'm more inclined to believe you were right all along when you voiced your fears about the possibility of another dirty cop. Considering I've only spoken directly to Lieutenant Finley, I have no choice but to believe he's another dirty cop working for Caruso."

Mallory's heart sank. If Jonah was right, they were in serious trouble.

Jonah could barely speak, he was so angry. He'd been betrayed by his boss! Finley was the one he'd called when someone had sneaked into his hospital room. Finley was the one who had ordered him to go after Mallory. And that story about no cops being available to relieve him was probably nothing more than a lie. Finley wanted him to stay put so he could send someone out to set the motel on fire.

Looking back, he realized how easily he'd been duped. Why would a boss send an injured cop out to keep a potential witness safe? If he'd been using the brain God gave him instead of relying on his emotions, he might have figured out Finley's true motives a lot quicker.

Mallory tightened her arms around his waist, giving him a warm hug that he felt all the way to the depths of his soul. "I'm sorry, Jonah."

He was amazed and humbled that she was trying to comfort him when he was the one who'd nearly gotten her killed. If not for the black Lab barking his head off, they might have succumbed to smoke inhalation.

God was truly watching over them.

"Mallory, I'm the one who should be apologizing to you," he said. "I should have been suspicious of Finley from the beginning. I'm sorry."

"We're safe on a train headed—somewhere far away from the burning motel, so there's no reason to apologize. You saved my life, Jonah. Twice. Three times, if you count forcing me to jump the train."

The way she chose to put a positive

spin on things was a personality quirk that surprised him. Time to take lessons from Mallory. This wasn't the time to wallow in self-pity about being duped by his boss. Mallory had made a good point about the train's destination—he had no clue where this train was headed. In the motel, when he'd first noticed the cargo train, he'd tried to do a search online to figure out where it was going. But the map wasn't any help. There were dozens of trains using the same tracks going in both directions. It was like looking at a freeway and trying to figure out where each car was going.

"Jonah, I can tell you're upset, and I wish you'd give yourself a break. Look how many miles we've already gone. The train is going at least fifteen or twenty miles per hour, right?" Once again, she sounded downright cheerful. "Your idea to jump the train was brilliant. We can ride for days if needed."

"Unfortunately, we can't afford to wait

that long. It's going to be dark soon and we need to get off before we lose all light. Keep an eye out for small towns, something not too far from the tracks since we have to walk."

He felt her sigh. "You think the bad guys will be waiting for us at the end of the line, huh?"

"I think it's a risk I'm not willing to take." He made sure his tone was firm. No way was he allowing her to talk him out of this one.

"Okay. Well, then, what about that place over there?"

There were lights just up ahead. For a minute he hesitated, worried that this town might be too easy to find. But maybe Caruso's men would assume they'd ride longer. After all, there were likely plenty of other towns along the way.

"Okay," he agreed, loosening his grip on her so he could turn and face the opening. As he scanned the area, looking for the best place to jump, he could feel Mallory edging closer behind him. He angled backward, so she could hear him better. "Do you want to go first?"

"Not really." She sounded less than enthused by the idea.

"There's no easy way to get off the train, just like there was no easy way to get on. You're going to hit the ground, so keep your muscles loose—don't tense up. Tuck your head and roll, going with the momentum instead of fighting against it. Understand?"

"Tuck and roll," she repeated faintly. "Got it."

He hated the way he kept putting her in danger but he had to stay focused on what needed to be done. Soon, very soon, he'd have her someplace safe. "Okay, watch me." For a moment he closed his eyes and prayed.

Please, Lord, keep us safe!

He opened his eyes and crouched low, so he was closer to the ground. Gauging the distance carefully, he sprang off the train like a broad jumper, trying to use his feet to break the force of impact on the ground before going limp and rolling, his momentum sending him through several rotations. As soon as he stopped, he jumped to his feet, sparing only a quick glance at his shirt. The open stitches in his incision weren't going to heal if he kept doing acrobatics like this. Trying to ignore the ache in his side, he searched for Mallory.

He heard her cry out before he saw her. She'd apparently jumped right after he did—he caught sight of her rolling across the grassy embankment.

"Mallory! Are you all right?" He ran to her and dropped to his knees. He quickly ran his hands over her arms and legs, hoping, praying she didn't have any broken bones.

"Lost—my—breath," she wheezed, as she stared up at the sky. "But I'm fine."

He dropped his chin to his chest. "Thank you, Lord," he murmured.

"Amen," Mallory added.

He jerked his head up to look at her. Was she poking fun at him? At God?

"Why are you looking at me like that?" she demanded. "I thought you were supposed to say *Amen* at the end of a prayer." She shifted uncomfortably and ran a shaky hand through her hair.

He nodded slowly. "Yes. You're right. But I thought you didn't believe in the power of prayer."

She shrugged and glanced away as if intensely interested in their surroundings. At least the open fields covered in high grass wouldn't make her claustrophobic the way the cornfields had. "Honestly, Jonah, I'm so confused right now, I'm not sure what I believe anymore. I find it hard to accept that simply believing in God will actually help us, yet on the other hand, every time Caruso seems to get close, we manage to get away, relatively unscathed. Are we just plain lucky? Or is God really watching over us, giving us strength?"

"God is really watching over us and giving us strength, Mallory. I promise if you open your heart and your mind, you'll be rewarded. And there's no risk to believing, right?"

"I'll try," she promised. She groaned a bit and then frowned as she staggered to her feet. "Hey, why does the town look farther away now than it did on the train?"

"Hopefully the walk won't be too bad." The town seemed farther away now that they were on solid ground. "If you're sure you're not hurt, we'd better get going. The earlier we check into the motel, the better."

"Why do you assume I'm hurt when you're the one recovering from surgery? Maybe you should take a look, make sure it's not bleeding."

"I'm sure it's fine." He glanced down and checked his dressing beneath his shirt, trying not to grimace at the dampness of blood. He was glad blood hadn't seeped onto his shirt since he didn't have a change of clothes. A bloody shirt might cause the motel clerk to become suspicious. "I'll get more gauze and tape tomorrow." In the big scheme of things, his injury was the least of his concerns.

Mallory gamely fell into step beside him. When their fingers brushed by accident, he curled his fingers into fists to keep himself from reaching for her hand, forcing himself to put more distance between them instead.

He might be stuck in the role of Mallory's protector, since he no longer trusted Finley—or anyone other than Gage for that matter—but he couldn't afford to get emotionally involved.

Not if he wanted to keep Mallory alive and safe from harm.

Mallory stifled a yawn as they made their way toward the lights of the town.

The adrenaline rush from jumping off the train had faded, big-time. She was tired and sore, and worst of all, she was keenly aware of Jonah walking beside her.

Just a few hours earlier, she'd begged him to let her stay. Now she'd gotten her wish, but they were on the run again. How could they investigate Caruso if they had to keep running? They didn't even have Jonah's computer anymore.

Jonah was holding himself distant now, as if this mess were somehow her fault, rather than his boss's fault. But on the train, he'd held her in his arms and she'd felt safe with a man for the first time in her entire life. She could have stayed there longer. Forever.

She told herself to be grateful for what she had. At least he wasn't turning her over to some strange cop. And he was probably just as tired and sore, too. No doubt his wound was bleeding again.

Maybe after they both got some rest, things would look better.

When they finally saw the neon sign for the motel, she wanted to weep with relief. She couldn't imagine sleeping outside with the bugs.

Jonah opened the door for her and then followed her inside. The desk clerk was an older, unshaven man with gray-streaked, greasy hair who leered at them as he chewed on the end of an unlit cigar. Jonah greeted him politely. "Good evening, my sister and I would like two connecting rooms, please."

"Your sister?" Cigar guy smirked, raking a rude gaze over her. "Yeah, sure. That'll cost you a hundred bucks."

Jonah smiled, as if he wasn't the least bit offended by the cigar guy's leering expression. "We'd like to spread the good word of God to all His people. Maybe you'll grant us a few minutes of your time?"

Cigar guy took a step back as if Jonah

carried some sort of contagious disease. "Fine—ninety bucks, and don't bother trying to convert me, Preacher Man. Leave me alone. Got it?"

"Thanks for your kind generosity." Jonah handed over the cash and picked up the two room keys. "God be with you, sir."

The clerk's terse "Good night" ended the conversation.

She waited until they were safely outside. "I can't believe you said that, Jonah. He almost refused to give us our rooms."

"It's a good cover, Mallory, and besides, I couldn't stand the way he was looking at you."

For a moment she was stunned speechless. She was dressed in a sweatshirt and jeans—why would the cigar guy notice her? Jonah's anger on her behalf humbled her. When was the last time a man had stood up for her honor?

Never.

When they found their rooms, Jonah

unlocked her door and flipped on the light. She flashed him a warm smile. "Thanks, Jonah, for everything."

He stared into her eyes, and for a tense second, she thought he was about to kiss her, but he abruptly turned away. "Make sure your side of the connecting door is unlocked, okay?"

She tried to hide the deep stab of disappointment. She should be glad Jonah hadn't tried to kiss her. "Okay."

"Good night, Mallory." Jonah unlocked his room and disappeared inside, closing the door quickly behind him before she could say anything.

Mallory took advantage of the facilities, enjoying the hot water against her sore muscles. But when she finally crawled into bed, she stared at the ceiling, unable to sleep.

She should be exhausted after running from a fire, jumping on a train, jumping off a train and walking for what seemed like miles. But her mind continued to race.

Should she try to pray? She closed her eyes and murmured the childhood prayer her parents had taught her, but saying the words as an adult felt silly, so she simply recited the Lord's Prayer.

Sleep continued to elude her. Her stomach was painfully empty and she sat up, reaching for her purse. She had a couple dollars, and she remembered there'd been a vending machine just outside the small office.

Jonah wouldn't like knowing she'd left the room, but the vending machine wasn't that far and she'd never get any sleep if she didn't eat something.

She pulled on her clothes, grabbed her room key and her money, and eased out the door. The area was only partially lit, as a few of the bulbs in the overhead lights were burned out.

She padded silently down the sidewalk and stood in front of the vending machine, trying to decide between the chocolate-chip cookies or the peanut-butter crackers. Finally, she bought both, smoothing the wrinkles from her dollar bills before feeding them into the slot of the machine.

"Well, now, looky here," a deep, nasally voice drawled. She froze as the cigar-chewing desk clerk came up close, invading her personal space so that she shrank back against the vending machine, the unyielding metal frame hard against her back. "If it isn't the pretty little preacher's *sister.*"

The cigar stench lacing his breath made her gag and for a moment she couldn't breathe, couldn't move as horrible memories of her past crowded into her mind. She opened her mouth but couldn't seem to make a sound.

"Let's say we have a little fun, huh?" He reached out to grab her and a flash of anger helped fuel her fighting instincts. She swept her arm up to block his hand, knocking his arm upward as she kicked the lower part of his stomach, her aim true.

Stunned by her attack, he doubled over, his eyes bulging and grunts of pain gurgling from his lips. When he didn't move, she grabbed her cookies and crackers from the bin of the vending machine and ran straight to her room.

There were several long seconds as she struggled to fit the key into the lock, but she managed to slip inside, locking the door securely behind her before she sank against the door frame, her whole body shaking with fear.

The entire incident had taken place with hardly any noise, since she hadn't managed to yell the way her Tae Kwon Do instructor had trained her to do. But at least she'd gotten away.

She couldn't believe cigar guy had come after her like that. She'd done nothing, *nothing* to provoke him.

For the first time in years, she was

forced to consider the possibility that maybe she hadn't done anything to provoke the sexual assault she'd suffered back when she was seventeen, either. After he'd assaulted her, Garrett Mason, the captain of the football team, had accused her of flirting with him. Of coming on to him. He'd told her that everything was her fault. And that no one would believe otherwise.

But now she wasn't so sure. Maybe some men, like Garrett and cigar man, were just evil, no matter how a woman looked or acted.

Right now, she was grateful she'd escaped. She closed her eyes and prayed. *Thank You, Lord, for keeping me safe.*

Opening her eyes, she was startled to feel a sense of peace. And she couldn't help but wonder if God had brought Jonah into her life to prove there were good men out there.

SIX

Jonah didn't sleep well, mostly because he kept thinking about Finley's betrayal. There was no doubt in his mind that his boss was working with Anthony Caruso. Why hadn't he figured it out sooner? No doubt Finley's plan all along was to send Jonah to find Mallory, and then once he had, send someone else to kill them both.

A plan that had almost succeeded.

The only issue was the timing of the ski-mask guy's arrival on the scene. Ski-mask guy had shown up at the cabin before Jonah had arrived so how could Finley have known where Mallory was hiding? Jonah thought back, piecing together a timeline of events. He'd stopped for dinner at Rose's Café in town and had casually asked about Mallory's uncle's place. Josie, the chatty woman behind the counter, had clued him in on where to find it. Was it possible Caruso's guy was there in the café, too? Had ski-mask guy overheard Josie giving him directions? It was the only way he could have beaten Jonah out there.

He tried to fit the pieces of the puzzle together. The only scenario that made sense was that the guy in the ski mask had planned to kill Mallory first, and then to hunker down and wait for Jonah to arrive. Luckily, ski-mask guy had underestimated Mallory's intelligence, strength and determination, just like Kent Wasserman had.

Jonah was more thankful than ever that he'd arrived just before Mallory burst out from the woods.

The minute the sun lightened the sky, he showered and headed over to the small lobby. The cigar-chewing clerk was just coming on duty, and when he caught sight of Jonah, he scowled.

"Checkout time is 11:00," he growled in his deep nasal tone.

"Thanks for letting me know," Jonah said graciously. "But we're thinking of staying another day."

"We don't got any rooms for you, Preacher Man."

"Really?" Jonah wasn't sure what this guy's problem was, but he wasn't about to get into the fight cigar guy was trying to start. He was glad he had his gun tucked in the back of his waistband, just in case. "That's interesting, because the sign outside says there's a vacancy."

The clerk reached out and flipped a switch on the wall next to him. Instantly the NO VACANCY light flashed on. "Not anymore."

Jonah hid a flash of anger. This guy was lying through his teeth, obviously willing to give up two paying customers to get rid of them. But why? Just because he'd claimed they were here to spread the word of God? He forced a smile. "I see. Well, then, my sister and I will make sure we're checked out by eleven. God be with you, sir."

The clerk only grunted in response and focused his attention on the small TV behind the counter. Jonah took several bagels from the continental breakfast buffet along with small packages of cream cheese and plastic knives, and went back to his room. He tentatively knocked on the connecting door. "Mallory? Are you awake? I have bagels for breakfast."

After a long minute, she unlocked the door. "Good morning, Jonah," she greeted him. Her hair was damp and curly from her recent shower.

The way she swept her gaze over the room, avoiding looking directly at him, caused him to frown. "Is there something wrong, Mallory?"

"No. Why do you ask?" Her gaze went up and to the right, a sure sign she wasn't being entirely truthful. In all his years of police work, he was amazed at how often people looked up and to the right when they were lying.

In a way, he didn't blame her for not trusting him. After all, he'd almost let his boss kill her in the motel fire. "Are you hungry?" he asked, gesturing to the food he'd brought from the lobby. "Please, help yourself. And if you're thirsty, there's orange juice, too. I'm happy to go back."

She crossed over and picked up a bagel, spreading a thin layer of cream cheese before taking a healthy bite. "I wouldn't mind some orange juice. Um— is that same desk clerk from last night working?" she asked.

He stared at her, dead certain her idle question was anything but casual. "Mallory, what happened?"

She flashed him a quick glance, full of guilt. "I don't know what you mean," she hedged.

Ignoring the bagel and his grumbling stomach, he crossed over to her, gently taking her slim shoulders in his hands. "Mallory, look at me. I can tell something is wrong. Why won't you tell me what happened?"

After a long pause, she reluctantly met his gaze. "Last night, I went out to get something to eat at the vending machine, and cigar guy tried to grab me, so I kicked him in the stomach." She flushed and looked away. "I'm not up to seeing him again, that's for sure."

Jonah tightened his grip on her shoulders, raking his gaze over her as if searching for signs of injury. "Are you all right?"

"I'm fine. I was quick enough that he didn't touch me." She twisted out of his grasp and took a step back.

A red haze covered his eyes and he was tempted to march back to confront cigar guy himself. No wonder he'd wanted them out—he knew Mallory could press assault charges against him. When Mallory sank into a chair, he struggled to remain calm as he faced her. "Why didn't you tell me?"

She stared at her half-eaten bagel. "There was no reason to bother you, Jonah. I told you, I can take care of myself. When he doubled over in pain, I ran back to my room. End of story."

Jonah knelt down beside her, forcing her to look at him. "The clerks have master keys to these rooms, Mallory. He might have come back to hurt you, or worse."

"I know," she said softly. "I actually thought of that, but he knew we had connecting rooms, remember? So after about an hour, I figured he was smart enough not to pursue anything further."

For a moment he closed his eyes, wishing he had the right to take Mallory into his arms, hold her close and never let go. But she was a key witness in his case, and he needed to remember that. Emotions had a way of clouding good judgment.

Besides, maybe she didn't want him holding her in his arms. Hadn't she faced cigar guy herself, without saying a word about it? If he hadn't pushed her for information, he still wouldn't have known what happened.

Which begged the question, what else hadn't Mallory told him?

Mallory looked down at Jonah's bowed head and resisted the urge to reach out and touch him. Last night, after she'd lain awake for over an hour, waiting for cigar man to come back, she'd wanted so badly to wake Jonah, seeking comfort. But she'd talked herself out of it.

She set her unfinished bagel aside, feeling slightly sick when she remembered what had transpired out at the vending machine. She felt bad Jonah was so upset about what had happened, but wasn't sure how to reassure him that it wasn't his fault.

"What can I do to earn your trust, Mallory?"

His question caught her off guard. "What do you mean? I trust you, Jonah. You're probably the only man in the world, aside from Gage, that I do trust."

He was slowly shaking his head. "No, you say that, Mallory, but deep down, you don't trust me. Be honest— you weren't going to say a word about what happened last night, were you? If I hadn't pushed the issue, you wouldn't have told me anything."

She let out a small sigh. "But that's not because I don't trust you, Jonah. I just didn't want to burden you with my problems. Especially when they aren't significant to solving our case."

"Listen carefully, Mallory. Everything that happens to you is important to me. *Everything.* I want you to promise me that you'll come to me no matter how insignificant you think your problem is. Promise?"

His obvious concern for her well-being warmed her heart. Looking into his chocolate-brown eyes, she couldn't refuse his request. "I promise."

"Good," he murmured, his gaze never wavering from hers. Once again, she had the sense he wanted to kiss her, but in an instant, the moment was gone. He rocked back on his heels and rose to his feet. He walked over to the small plate of bagels. "After we're finished with breakfast, we'll have to find some sort of transportation out of here."

"We're leaving?" She was surprised Jonah didn't want to stay another day.

Jonah swallowed his food before answering. "Cigar guy has no intention of renting us rooms for another night. After what you told me, there's no way I'd agree to stay anyway."

"But what sort of transportation are we going to find here, in a small town?"

"I don't know, but I'm convinced we'll find something."

* * *

That something ended up being a small motorcycle that was propped near the street with a crudely written for-sale sign taped to it. Mallory watched as Jonah spoke to the guy selling the bike, and then started it up, to make sure the thing worked.

"Are you crazy?" she said under her breath. "We're going to run out of cash."

"Don't worry. I'll ask Gage to wire us some. Besides, this is a great deal." The broad grin on his face made her want to roll her eyes.

What was that saying? Something about men and their toys? Honestly, he looked like a little kid on Christmas morning, grinning from ear to ear as he straddled the bike and plunked a helmet on his head. "Come on, it'll be fun."

His idea of fun was very different from hers, but she took the second helmet and put it on her head, tucking in her hair. When she was ready, she climbed on the small seat behind him. "Are you sure you know how to drive this thing?"

"Ye of little faith," he scoffed. "Hang on!" Jonah revved the motor and then took off down the street. She gasped when she slipped backward in the seat, and clung tightly to his waist.

As they sped out of town, she was reminded of how he'd held her in his arms as they had ridden the train.

This was just as nice, she decided, as she leaned against Jonah's strong back and lifted her face to the wind. For a short while, she could pretend they were simply out for a ride, enjoying being together as the miles flew by.

Jonah took several different highways, heading toward Chicago. He hadn't ridden a motorcycle since he and Gage were in high school, and he couldn't deny he was having fun.

And he was far too aware of Mallory's arms wrapped tightly around his waist.

Every two hours they had to stop for gas to fill the motorcycle's small fuel tank. But they soon crossed the state line into Illinois.

At the gas station, he broke a twenty to use for the tolls. When Mallory groaned under her breath as she climbed on the back of the bike, he decided he'd find a place to stay outside of Chicago.

"Just another hour," he promised.

This time, he chose a nicer motel, one that boasted a small business center, which meant they'd have some computer access. He was glad there wasn't a sleazy motel clerk behind the counter this time, as he asked for two connecting rooms.

"Is there a fee for using the internet on the lobby computer?" he asked as he signed in as Jonah Adams and paid cash for the two rooms.

"Nope, but I'll kick you off if I catch you surfing anything inappropriate," the clerk said.

"No problem," he said quickly. "I just want to catch up on the latest news, that's all."

"Would you mind if I buy a T-shirt from the mini-mart across the street?" Mallory asked. "I've been wearing this same sweatshirt for two days."

Jonah hesitated, not liking the thought of letting her out of his sight, even for an hour of shopping. But no one knew where they were, not even Gage. He decided to take the risk.

Jonah took out his wallet. "Here, buy some stuff for both of us and we'll wash these clothes in the laundry facilities. Get some more gauze and tape, too. And a disposable cell phone."

"Anything else?" she asked drily.

"No, that should cover it." He handed her the cash he had and was glad she didn't argue about taking it.

"I'll be back soon."

"Good. I'll be here on the computer, waiting for you." When Mallory turned to go, he had to stop himself from reaching out for her. Letting her walk away alone was difficult.

The first thing he did online was send Gage a quick email, letting his buddy know they were safe but unavailable by phone. He'd left his cell behind when they'd escaped from the motel fire. Besides, he wouldn't use his old cell phone anyway, knowing Finley had the ability to track it down.

He quickly explained his suspicions about Finley to Gage and warned his buddy not to go to the police for anything regarding this case. Jonah was surprised when he received a return email from Gage within fifteen minutes. Gage offered to wire him some money and Jonah agreed, making the necessary arrangements.

Once he'd gotten that out of the way, Jonah started reviewing the *Chicago Tribune* headlines. He scanned all the articles that even remotely discussed politics, but didn't find much information on Anthony Caruso.

He typed in both Caruso's name along with Bernardo Salvatore's name and got a hit. A newspaper article from three months ago mentioned briefly how Caruso was eating dinner at Salvatore's newest restaurant.

Jonah frowned when the article mentioned how Caruso was escorting a young model named Claire Richmond. When he blew up the photograph, he was shocked to realize Claire Richmond was tall, slender and had blond hair and blue eyes, just like Mallory.

Did Mallory know about the other women in Caruso's life? Or had Caruso already broken up with Claire Richmond by the time he'd met Mallory?

Somehow, he doubted it. He decided to do another search with both Claire Richmond and Anthony Caruso's names linked together, and dozens of articles came up.

His opinion of Caruso wasn't getting any better, that was for sure.

Jonah found several photos of Claire and Anthony together at various outings, but none of them recent. All the photographs were taken three to four months ago. Grudgingly he was forced to admit that it was possible Caruso hadn't been two-timing Mallory.

Still, he found himself wanting to show Mallory what he'd found. Ridiculous, really, because he doubted Mallory had any secret feelings for the man who was trying to kill her.

Jonah glanced at his watch. Where was Mallory? She should be back by now. How long did it take to buy a few articles of clothing?

He was tempted to go out looking for her, but an article caught his eyes in his search list as he scrolled down a few.

Missing Model: Runaway? Or Foul Play?

Missing? His gut knotted as he clicked on the link. The date on the article was just a month ago. Right about the time Mallory claimed she and Anthony Caruso had started dating.

He leaned forward and began to read.

Claire Richmond had everything going for her: a million-dollar contract with Sports International and a powerful, handsome state senator as an escort. But less than two months after her breakup with Anthony Caruso, Claire Richmond disappeared. Her friends say she was heartbroken when Anthony broke off their relationship, despite the way she'd always put on a brave front. But she failed to show up for a photo shoot and was reported missing.

Now that she's been gone more than five weeks, the police are starting to wonder if Claire Richmond ran away from the spotlight and the endless questions about her broken relationship with the senator, or if her disappearance is the result of foul play.

The small hairs on the back of his neck lifted as he read the article twice, making sure he didn't miss anything.

This couldn't be a coincidence.

"Hey, I didn't think you'd still be here," Mallory said, as she came into the lobby.

He turned to look at her, noting she was wearing fresh clothes. The bright orange T-shirt and jeans were nothing fancy, but Mallory was beautiful no matter what she wore.

"I was getting worried," he admitted slowly.

"Silly. I was perfectly fine." She frowned as she glanced over his shoulder at the computer screen. "Who's that?"

For a split second, he considered not

sharing what he'd found. But he'd asked for her trust, so he needed to offer the same. "You'd better sit down, Mallory."

The color drained from her cheeks.

He glanced over to make sure the clerk wasn't paying attention. Thankfully, she was on the phone taking a reservation. "This woman is Claire Richmond, a young model who happened to be dumped by Anthony Caruso just a few months ago. She's been missing for the past five weeks."

Mallory stared at the photo in shock. He waited as she quickly scanned the article.

He put his hand on hers. "Mallory, I think Caruso had something to do with her disappearance."

Mallory turned toward Jonah and opened her mouth to speak just as she began to faint.

SEVEN

Jonah reached out and caught Mallory, lowering her into the chair beside him. "She looks like me," she whispered.

"Not really," he murmured reassuringly, although he couldn't deny there was a resemblance. "This other woman only slightly looks like you. And that doesn't mean anything other than Caruso obviously prefers to date beautiful blondes."

Her gaze remained troubled. "I don't understand. Do you think it's possible she stumbled across proof that Anthony was involved in something illegal, just like I did?"

"I don't know," Jonah admitted. "If that's true, it doesn't make sense that he'd wait almost two months after the breakup to get rid of her." He looked up Claire Richmond's last known address and then deleted the cache before he shut down the computer. "Come on, we need to get back to our rooms."

He put a supporting arm around her waist as they headed outside. Mallory walked beside him as if she were lost in a fog, her gaze unfocused and her breathing shallow. Maybe he shouldn't have told her about Claire Richmond.

He unlocked the door to his room and she immediately sank into the closest seat. After unlocking the connecting door between their rooms, he hesitated in the doorway and glanced back at her. "You did buy the disposable cell phone, right?"

She nodded. Turning his attention back to her room, he spied the bags sitting on her bed, the disposable phone sitting right on top. He grabbed the phone and returned to his room. Using the phone-book map, he pinpointed Claire's address.

"Who are you calling?" Mallory asked. Her voice was stronger and she looked a little less as if she was going to throw up. He was reminded again how Mallory was much stronger than she looked.

"The Chicago P.D. I'm going to find out what district is handling Claire's case and then I'm going to chat with the detective in charge."

She shook her head slowly. "You really think her disappearance is related to the Jefferson Project?"

"Claire's disappearance might not be related directly to the Jefferson Project per se, but I do think Caruso had something to do with it. For all we know, he's involved with other illegal ventures. Claire could have stumbled across something incriminating, like you said." Or simply been in the wrong place at the wrong time. He stared down at the map of the city, where he'd made a star at the point of her address. "I just can't believe her disappearance is a coincidence. And since our leads are few and far between, I think we need to probe further."

"But the article didn't say anything about Caruso being a suspect," Mallory argued.

"No, it didn't, which is why I want to talk to the detective in charge. Could be that Caruso's a person of interest in the case but that they don't have any evidence against him. Or that he has some sort of ironclad alibi." Depressing thought, but highly likely—Caruso wasn't the type to do his own dirty work. Hadn't he proved that by sending thugs after Mallory? He flipped open the phone and dialed.

It took him almost ten minutes of being transferred from one department to the next before he finally reached Detective Nick Butler.

"Detective Butler? My name is Detective Jonah Stewart and I work in Milwaukee's district six. We have a missing-person case here, a woman by the name of Mallory Roth. She's a young blonde who happened to be dating Senator Caruso just before she disappeared. I noticed you have a similar case involving the disappearance of Claire Richmond, so I wanted to talk to you in person."

"Stewart?" Jonah could hear computer keys tapping in the background. "What's your badge number?"

Jonah rattled it off, even though the last thing he wanted was for Butler to call and validate his identity with Finley. "Look, before you call the district to prove I really am MPD, you need to know my life is in danger. At the moment, I'm working off-grid."

There was a short pause. "How quickly can you get to Chicago?" Butler asked.

"Forty minutes."

Butler wisely didn't bother asking for

specifics about his location. "Okay, let's say we meet in an hour at the coffee shop across the street from my district. I won't make any calls yet but make sure you bring your badge."

"An hour," he repeated. "Thanks. I really appreciate this." He shut the phone with a satisfied snap.

"Did you have to give him my name?" Mallory asked with a frown. "I mean, don't you think it's going to make us look bad when we meet him?"

He slowly turned to face her, knowing she wasn't going to like what he was planning. "You're not coming, Mallory. The only way I can pull this off is if I convince Butler that I'm investigating a missing person whose disappearance could be linked to his case. I need him to share what he knows, cop to cop, and I'll have to give him some information in return while pretending I haven't found you yet."

Her gaze narrowed. "An hour ago, you

didn't want me to go shopping alone, but now you're just going to ride off to Chicago by yourself?"

He went over to kneel beside her chair so they were at eye level. "Mallory, I know you're upset, and if I could bring you along, I would. But this is important. We need whatever information Butler has about Caruso."

"And what if he doesn't have any information? This could be nothing more than a wild-goose chase."

"It's possible, but I think the Chicago P.D. has at least considered him a suspect at one point or another. So I can guarantee this trip won't be a waste of time. Just stay here and stay safe, okay? Please? For me?"

She let out her breath in a heavy sigh. "It's not like I have much of a choice, right?"

"I'll be back as soon as possible." Before he could stop himself, he pulled her into his arms in a quick hug. Once he realized he'd crossed the line, he hastily let her go and stood. "Don't open the door to anyone but me," he said as he grabbed his helmet and keys.

He avoided her gaze, leaving the motel room before she could say anything more. He jammed his helmet onto his head, telling himself he was an idiot.

He couldn't afford to get close to Mallory on an emotional level.

But he was beginning to fear that he already had.

Mallory imagined she could still smell Jonah's scent clinging to her new T-shirt long after he was gone.

She buried her face in her hands. She'd wanted to stay in his arms, to revel in his tender strength. Tears pricked her eyes and the small sign of weakness was enough to spur her into action.

She bounded to her feet. She would not cry over a man. Any man. Even one as nice as Jonah.

Returning to her room, she busied herself with unpacking the rest of the items she'd purchased, putting everything away.

Except for the second disposable cell phone.

Refusing to feel guilty for not telling Jonah she'd purchased two—after all, she'd used her own money for the second phone—she sat on the edge of her bed and began to dial Alyssa's number. Alyssa must have replaced her phone by now. She left a message, hoping Alyssa would get it.

Unfortunately, Mallory didn't know Gage's number by memory.

She hated not knowing what was going on with her twin. Was Alyssa all finished with surgery? Had everything gone well? She and Jonah had spent so much time running away from danger she'd barely had time to think about Alyssa.

After jumping to her feet, Mallory

began to pace. She wasn't going to sit here and do nothing while she waited for Jonah. There had to be something she could do to help.

Maybe she should try to remember more details about the night of the charity event at the Pfister Hotel. If only she knew more about the people Caruso spoke to on a regular basis. But he didn't have a lot of family, his parents were dead, and he was divorced from his first wife and didn't have kids. Or so he claimed.

Wait a minute, what about his first wife? Was it possible she knew something? And if so, was she still in the Chicago area?

Mallory headed back to the lobby but there was a short, balding man seated at the computer, printing his airline boarding pass. She crossed her arms and tapped her foot impatiently. When he finally finished, she swooped in on the computer.

She found searching for people's names online wasn't as easy as Jonah made it look. But after fifteen minutes, she found the full name of Anthony's first wife— Rachel Camille Simon, a thirty-six-year-old blonde who just happened to be the heiress to the Simon estate. Her father was George Simon, the founder of the Simon Corporation, which had several diverse interests from pharmaceuticals to insurance.

Further searching revealed Rachel Camille Simon was following in her father's footsteps, working her way up in the company. Her pulse skipped with excitement when she realized the Simon headquarters was only about twenty minutes from the motel.

She wanted to talk to Anthony's first wife, but the woman was second in command at a multibillion-dollar corporation. What was she going to do, waltz in and demand to speak directly to Rachel? She'd be lucky to get two steps into the building before the security guards hauled her out of there, kicking and screaming. No, she needed to figure out a way to contact Rachel first and somehow convince the woman to at least talk to her. But how?

She went back to her room, called the general number for the Simon Corporation and asked to speak to Rachel Simon's assistant. "And what is the nature of your call?" the woman asked.

"I'm sorry, but it's personal."

There was a long pause, and Mallory was afraid the woman was going to refuse to put her through, but then the next thing she knew another woman was answering the phone. "Good afternoon, Edith Goodman speaking. How may I direct your call?"

"Ms. Goodman, my name is Mallory Roth and I need to speak to Ms. Simon about a personal matter that involves her ex-husband, Senator Caruso."

"I'm sorry, but Ms. Simon doesn't

speak to reporters." The woman's friendly tone had cooled considerably.

"Wait! Don't hang up. I promise I'm not a reporter. I'm from Milwaukee, and I'm in danger. I believe her ex-husband is trying to kill me."

This time, the pause was even longer. Mallory figured it was a fifty-fifty chance that she'd be passed off as some kook or put through to Rachel's office. Finally Edith said, "I'll take your name and number and let Ms. Simon decide whether or not she'll call you back."

The answer was better than what she'd hoped for. She quickly rattled off her name and her new cell-phone number. "Thank you, Ms. Goodman, very much."

Mallory sighed and stared down at the phone in her hand. In truth, contacting Caruso's first wife was a total long shot. For all she knew, Caruso hadn't even gone down the path of corruption until after his divorce. Rachel might tell her she was crazy to believe her ex-husband would hurt a fly.

She tossed the phone on the bed and raked her fingers through her hair. How long had Jonah been gone? She checked the small alarm clock and winced. Not long. He wouldn't be back for hours yet.

She turned on the television, switching channels until she found the news. When her phone rang twenty minutes later, she was so startled she almost fell off the bed.

Her heart pounding, she grabbed the phone and flipped it open. On the screen she could see the caller was using a blocked number. Hesitantly, she answered, "Hello?"

"Is this Mallory Roth?" a female voice asked.

"Yes." She closed her eyes and pumped her hand in the air. Caruso's ex had returned her call! "Thank you so much for calling me back, Ms. Simon. I know you're very busy, but I desperately need to talk to you."

"You told my assistant that you feared for your life. Is that true?"

"Yes, Ms. Simon. It's true. I believe Anthony Caruso has already sent two hit men to kill me and I'm afraid he won't stop until he's succeeded."

There was a brief pause. "All right, I'll make time to meet you. But I'm warning you, if this is some sort of trick, I'll bury you so deep in lawsuits you'll never get out."

Mallory was light-headed with relief. "Agreed. I promise I'm not a reporter. Where would you like to meet?"

"Crabapple Park, at the merry-go-round. It's located about five miles northeast of our corporate office."

Mallory scribbled down the directions. "Okay, I'll see you there in thirty minutes." She scooped her purse off the bed and ran out of the motel toward the office to request a taxi.

If Rachel Simon agreed to the meeting, that meant she knew something about how dangerous her ex- husband was. Rachel hadn't sounded too surprised to hear Mallory feared for her life. Mallory could only hope that her meeting was just as productive as Jonah's.

And that she'd beat him back to the motel. It wasn't until she was almost all the way to the park that she realized she should have left Jonah a note.

Jonah stared at the report detailing Claire Richmond's investigation as Nick Butler downed the last of his coffee. The Chicago detective was in his late thirties and reminded Jonah far too much of Drew. He finished the report and sighed. "Just as I figured—he has the perfect alibi."

"Yeah, we called every person on his list to validate his story," Butler agreed. "We're pretty certain he could be involved, but there's been no way to prove it."

"Would a second missing person help?" Jonah asked. He began to fold his copy of the report, as Butler had agreed that he could keep it.

"Depends on what information you've found in the course of your investigation. We had to tiptoe around Caruso the first time, because he's a state senator."

"I'm afraid I don't have much," Jonah confessed. Sensing Nick's growing impatience with the one-sided flow of information, he decided to give him what he could. "But we believe Caruso may be involved in money laundering in addition to attempted murder. We have two dead men, Hugh Jefferson and Eric Holden, who were both huge financial contributors to Caruso's last campaign. We have reason to believe they were involved in the money-laundering scheme, too. In fact, we think Caruso was the man in charge."

"Really?" Nick Butler's eyes had brightened with the news.

"I'm afraid I don't have a lot more, other than what I have already told you. They had at least one dirty cop working for them, and all three died in a fire on Jefferson's yacht. Just a few days before they all died, Mallory Roth went missing."

Nick leaned closer. "Do you really think you have a dirty cop still working for Caruso?"

"Yeah, I do. I went searching for Mallory Roth and the only person I'd been in contact with was my boss. I told him I had found her, and suddenly our motel is set on fire, the doors locked from the outside." Jonah didn't even like thinking about how close they'd come to dying that night. "We made it out alive, but I've obviously cut off all communications with him."

"Dirty cops make me sick," Nick muttered with a scowl. "But you found Mallory Roth?"

"Yeah, but I want to keep that information low-key for now. At this point we only have her word against his." Jonah wrote his new cell-phone number on a napkin and pushed it across the table. "If you find out anything else, will you call me? And I'll keep you in the loop of my investigation, too."

"Sure thing." Butler stuffed the napkin in the front pocket of his shirt. "I wish you luck, Stewart. If we're both right, Caruso's a slippery one. It's not going to be easy to take him down."

"I know." Jonah rose to his feet and held out his hand. "Take care."

Jonah straddled his motorcycle and started the engine. He hoped the traffic wasn't too bad—he was sure Mallory wouldn't be happy that he was gone so long.

But the trip hadn't been a total waste. For one thing, Nick had confirmed his suspicions that they'd considered Caruso a possible suspect. And that Caruso had been out of town in Washington D.C. during the twenty-four-hour time frame when Claire had disappeared.

So while he didn't find out a lot of new information, he felt as if they were on the right track.

He made good time getting back to the motel. As he drove into the parking space right in front of their rooms, he frowned when he noticed Mallory's window was dark. He could just make out the flickering light from the TV.

After parking his bike, he opened his door and pulled off his helmet as he strode to the open doorway between their rooms. "Mallory?"

No answer. He flipped on a light so he could see, even though it wasn't quite dark outside yet. He poked his head in the bathroom. No sign of Mallory.

He stood in the middle of the room, sweeping his gaze over her belongings.

The bags from her recent purchases were still scattered on her bed, but her purse was gone.

Helpless panic surged. Where was she? Had she left on her own? Or had Caruso found her after all?

He never should have left her alone. Never.

EIGHT

Mallory's taxi driver dropped her off outside of Crabapple Park. She tipped him and asked for his card so she could call him when she was finished. Trying to look carefree, she ambled through the park, circling the merry-go-round twice before a woman dressed casually in jeans and a pink hoodie sweatshirt approached. "Are you Mallory Roth?"

Her heart sank as she turned to face the woman. She had blonde hair, but wasn't dressed in the corporate suit she'd expect of a VP. Rachel Simon must have sent someone in her place. "Yes, I'm Mallory."

There was a slight hesitation before the woman formally held out her hand.

"I'm Rachel Simon. I believe you wanted to speak with me?"

Mallory stared at her for a moment, not sure if this woman was really Rachel or if this was some trick. "I'm sorry, but do you have your ID handy?"

There was a flash of annoyance, but Rachel obliged her. "I changed my clothes in case I was followed."

Looking past the clothes, the woman did resemble the photo on the internet, so she decided to trust her. "I would like to speak with you. Could we sit down?"

"Of course." Rachel Simon led the way over to an isolated park bench. She sat down at an angle so they could see each other as they spoke.

Now that she was face-to-face with Caruso's ex-wife, Mallory wasn't sure where to begin. She wished she'd waited for Jonah. What on earth made her think she could play detective? "I'm sorry, but I don't know where to begin."

"Why don't you start by telling me

why Anthony wants to kill you?" Rachel bluntly asked.

Okay, then. "Because I overheard him discussing how to cover up a murder," Mallory admitted. "I was hoping you could explain why you divorced him."

Rachel shrugged and glanced away. "Suffice it to say we didn't want the same things out of life."

Mallory narrowed her gaze, her mind racing. Clearly Caruso's ex wasn't going to give him up easily. "Look, Ms. Simon, I'm in trouble. Caruso has already tried to frame me for murder, and he'll keep trying to kill me if I can't come up with some proof to use against him in court. Proof that he's involved in something illegal. So let's be honest with each other, okay? Did you divorce him because of his involvement with money laundering?"

"Money laundering?" The surprise in Rachel's dark eyes was all too real. She shook her head. "No, he must have gotten involved with that after we went our separate ways. Although I honestly can't say that I'm surprised."

A flicker of hope made her lean forward eagerly. "Why aren't you surprised? Did you discover other illegal activities he was involved in?"

There was a long silence as Rachel Simon stared down at her clasped hands. "Yes, you could say that," she finally admitted. "I discovered that some of the high-powered supporters of his campaign had connections with organized crime. When I confronted Anthony, he laughed and told me to mind my own business."

"Did he try to hurt you?" Mallory asked, suspecting there was far more to the story than Rachel was letting on.

"I was afraid he might, so I went to my father's lawyer, who helped me put together an agreement that Anthony couldn't refuse. I'd stay silent about what

I'd discovered if he'd grant me a divorce. Anthony wisely agreed to the terms."

The flicker of hope died. "So you can't help me."

Rachel smoothed out a wrinkle in her jeans. "I've kept silent all these years but after that woman disappeared, I began to wonder if it was worth it."

"You mean Claire Richmond?"

Rachel nodded. "One day, her body will be found but there won't be a shred of evidence linking her death to Anthony." Her tone was full of bitterness.

"How do you know he's involved?" Mallory asked. "I mean, suspecting him is one thing, but you would have had to see something to know for certain."

"I know because Anthony told me." Rachel lifted her head and looked Mallory straight in the eye. "Once the media picked up on her disappearance, I received a bouquet of red roses. The card read, 'If you ever break your promise, the same thing will happen to you and those you love.'"

Mallory sucked in a harsh breath. "He threatened you?"

"Oh, yes, he threatened me. And I believe him." Rachel stared over at the merry-go-round, where kids were squealing with joy. "Marrying Anthony Caruso was the biggest mistake I've ever made in my life. And even though we're divorced, I'll never be free of him. *Never.*"

"That's not true," Mallory said as she reached over to lightly clasp Rachel's arm. "You can be free of him. All we need to do is to find enough proof to get Caruso arrested. You need to work with us on this."

"Us?" Rachel tore her arm away and jumped to her feet, her accusing gaze harsh. "I thought you were alone. You didn't say anything about working with someone else."

Recognizing the stark fear in Rachel's

eyes, she held out her hand in an effort to calm her down as she slowly rose to her feet. "I was saved from Caruso's thug by a Milwaukee police detective named Jonah Stewart. But he's not here now, and he doesn't know I'm meeting with you. I promise you, he doesn't know I'm here."

"I shouldn't have come," Rachel muttered, running a hand through her hair. "I'm sorry, but I can't help you."

"Wait! Please don't go. Don't you realize there's strength in numbers? Maybe you and I can't take Caruso down by ourselves, but together we can do this."

But Rachel was already shaking her head. "You don't understand. We have a nine-year-old son, Joey. Even if I wanted to help you, I couldn't. I'd never risk anything happening to my son. I'm afraid you'll have to find your evidence against Anthony without me."

"But—" Mallory watched helplessly

as Rachel turned and began walking away. "Please, don't go!"

Abruptly, Rachel stopped and turned back to face Mallory. "Whatever you decide to do, be careful. Anthony is ruthless. You were right when you said he'd keep after you until he succeeded. He is not a man to mess with. But know this—if you repeat any part of this conversation to the authorities, I'll deny every word. I have staff members who will testify that I've been in a meeting with them during this exact time frame."

Mallory's shoulders slumped with dejection. Rachel might have agreed to meet with her out of pity, but she wasn't going to allow herself to become involved. And after learning about her son, Mallory couldn't really blame her.

Anthony hadn't told her about his son.

"I understand, Rachel. But please, if you change your mind, call me. You have my number, right? I promise we would do everything possible to keep you and your son safe."

"Don't hold your breath," Rachel advised before she turned and walked away.

Mallory let her go, her stomach knotted with despair. She'd probably blown the one chance they had to get the proof they needed to take down Caruso. And there was nothing she could do about it, except go back and tell Jonah what happened.

And hope he could find a way to forgive her.

The lights were blazing from her room as well as Jonah's when the taxi driver let her out in front of the hotel. For a moment she was tempted to jump back in to go somewhere else—anywhere but here.

Reminding herself she wasn't a coward, she paid the driver and then used her key to open the door. The minute she entered the room, Jonah came rushing through the open connecting doors, his eyes wild. "Are you okay? What happened? Where have you been?"

Knowing he was worried about her safety made her feel even worse. "I'm fine," she hastened to reassure him. "I'm sorry I forgot to leave a note."

Jonah raked a gaze over her, as if to check that she was really okay, before he crossed his arms about his chest and glared at her. "You shouldn't have gone anywhere at all. What part of *being safe* don't you understand, Mallory? Do you have any idea what I've been going through?"

"I already apologized," she reminded him, keeping her tone even with an effort. "And yelling at me isn't going to change what happened. If it makes you feel any better, I know I was wrong. And I won't make the same mistake again."

"What happened? You look upset." Instantly, his anger turned to concern.

She dropped into a chair and sighed.

"I went to meet with Caruso's ex-wife. She knows he's involved with something illegal, but she won't help us."

Jonah couldn't have looked any more flabbergasted. "Caruso's ex-wife? I didn't even know he had an ex-wife!"

"He happened to mention his divorce, shortly after we first met," she admitted. "And they've been divorced for a long time, almost ten years. Apparently she promised to keep his secret if he granted her a divorce."

"And you expect me to believe Caruso went along with it?" Jonah scoffed. "I doubt it. He'd just silence her the way he has silenced everyone else who crossed him."

"Her family is wealthy and powerful. He probably knew their word would carry a lot of credibility."

Jonah stared at her for a long moment. "What's her name?"

"Rachel Camille Simon. And before you think you can leverage her cooperation where I failed, you should probably know they have a son. And she's convinced Caruso would kill his own son if he even suspected she broke her promise." When Jonah scrubbed his hands over his face, she knew just how he felt. Her clue had only led them to a dead end. "So, how did your meeting with the Chicago P.D. go?"

"About as good as yours," he said drily. "They have suspicions that Caruso is involved in Claire's disappearance, but no proof."

"So what should we do now?"

Jonah sighed. "I say we go out for dinner."

"Dinner?" she echoed incredulously. "That's it? We just go out for dinner?"

"We're going to eat at Salvatore's restaurant, in downtown Chicago. It's the only other link we have to Caruso at this point. And besides, I'm hungry."

Jonah's pulse still hadn't settled down by the time they'd arrived at the restaurant. He couldn't believe Mallory had actually gone off to talk to Caruso's ex-wife without telling him. Or waiting for him.

"Oh, look, outside seating." Mallory pulled off her helmet and ran her fingers through her hair. "It's a beautiful night."

"Actually, I'd rather sit inside. It's our best chance to find out something about the owner himself, Bernardo Salvatore," he said.

She shrugged but didn't say anything more as they walked inside. Thankfully, the place wasn't too fancy, although the food smelled heavenly. "This way," the hostess said in a soft Sicilian accent.

"Does Mr. Salvatore himself ever eat here?" Jonah asked as she stood by a small table for two and waited for them to take their seats. "I would love to meet him sometime."

The hostess's expression remained neutral, although he sensed she wasn't entirely pleased by his question. "Mr. Salvatore is very busy, but yes, he does occasionally stop in for dinner, although he prefers to be left alone." She quickly went on to describe the specials for the evening, and Jonah couldn't help but find her reaction curious.

Once the hostess left, Mallory leaned forward. "That was a little strange," she whispered. "I got the impression she was warning us off."

"Yeah, I know." Jonah glanced at the menu, wincing a little at the prices. They were getting low on cash. Even though Gage had agreed to get him more, he couldn't help wondering if this was a bad idea. What could they learn from eating here? He considered getting up to leave, but decided that would only fuel any suspicions the hostess already had. "What would you like to eat?"

"Spaghetti and meatballs," Mallory said, picking one of the cheaper items on the menu. "I'm in the mood for comfort food."

"Sounds good."

The server came by and introduced herself as Kate. She was young, blonde and slender, reminding him a bit of Claire Richmond. After she took their order, he flashed a warm smile and went with his gut. "Did you know Claire Richmond? She's an old friend of ours. She used to work here, right? Before she landed her big modeling contract?"

Kate's bright smile dimmed and a hint of alarm flashed in her eyes. "Uh, no, I didn't know Claire."

"But she used to work here, didn't she?" he persisted, instinctively knowing he was on the right track.

Her gaze was a bit uncertain, as if she wasn't sure what to say, but then she shook her head. "I don't know. Excuse me but I need to place your order with the kitchen." The waitress couldn't get away from their table fast enough.

"How did you know Claire Richmond worked here?" Mallory asked in a low voice.

He shrugged and grinned wryly. "Lucky guess. Where else would a twenty-one-year-old meet a man like Caruso? And land a big modeling contract?"

"She looked scared," Mallory murmured, staring at the door Kate had disappeared through. "Maybe you should have told her you're a cop."

Jonah knew that sometimes people were more likely to open up to someone outside of law enforcement. "I'd rather pretend to be a concerned friend of the family."

Their dinner arrived in record time, and Jonah tried to catch the gaze of the young man who brought their food, but he simply dropped the plates and left. No one stopped by to offer freshly grated Parmesan cheese or ask how their meal was, which he also found very peculiar. Apparently, the management at Salvatore's was anxious to get rid of them because he'd asked too many questions.

Kate didn't return until they'd finished their meal. "Hope everything was all right. Are you interested in dessert?"

He looked at Mallory, who shook her head. "No thanks. Just the check, please."

"Certainly." Kate's perky smile and cheerful attitude were back in place, as if nothing had transpired earlier. But when she brought over the vinyl case holding their bill, she leaned close. "Abby knew Claire—she'll be outside," she whispered, before adding at a normal volume, "You can pay me whenever you're ready. Thanks for dining with us this evening."

"We enjoyed our meal, didn't we, honey?" he asked, beaming at Mallory like a devoted boyfriend. He placed cash in the vinyl folder and pushed it toward Kate.

"Absolutely." Mallory played along. "I'm so thrilled they're opening up a Salvatore's at home, aren't you?"

He quickly nodded. "Can't wait."

"Thanks again," Kate said as she walked away.

He stood and placed his hand against Mallory's back as she led the way outside. There were swarms of people crowding the sidewalks, so he stepped up against the building, glancing around for someone who apparently was willing to talk to them.

"Over there," Mallory murmured, nudging him. "She's staring at us."

Sure enough, a young brunette was standing across the street, smoking a cigarette and trying to catch their attention. "Let's go," he said to Mallory.

Mallory took his arm as they walked toward the waitress, keeping up the pretense of being out on a date. "Abby?" she asked as they approached.

The brunette crushed out the cigarette. "Next time, use a little finesse. We don't talk about Claire in the restaurant. Ever."

"I'm sorry," he apologized quickly. "I

should have been more subtle. We're just very anxious to find our friend. When was the last time you spoke to her?"

She gave him a disgusted look. "Drop the act. You're obviously a cop. I can spot one a mile away. I don't know what you think you're doing, but Claire is gone and she's never coming back. I spoke to her the night before she disappeared. Her plan was to go to the police with what she knew and then cash in the expensive jewelry he'd given her to relocate somewhere else, but then she was gone. Poof. Vanished. As if she'd never been here."

He couldn't believe she was telling them all this. "How do you know she didn't disappear on her own?"

"Because she was going to wait until after the weekend, since Friday and Saturday night are the highest-paying shifts." Abby looked at Jonah as if he were stupid.

That didn't make sense. "Why would

she need to wait tables? I thought she had a big modeling contract."

Abby glanced away and shrugged. "She didn't think modeling was going to work out long-term."

Interesting. Had Caruso threatened to take the contract away?

"Did she say exactly what she wanted to say to the police?"

"No. And I didn't ask."

"Have you mentioned at least this much to the police?" Mallory piped up. "Do they know she was going to come to talk to them?"

"Yeah, right." Abby let out a harsh laugh. "You don't cross Salvatore or any of his friends. I need my job so don't ever come into the restaurant asking about Claire again. Understand? It's not exactly healthy, if you know what I mean."

Before he could thank her, she disappeared into the crowd of pedestrians.

"I don't like this, Jonah," Mallory murmured. "They're all so scared."

"She didn't give us much information.

She never mentioned Caruso's name—she only referred to Salvatore's friends." He tried to ignore the surge of hopelessness. All of their leads were just dead ends.

"I hope we didn't cause either Abby or Kate any trouble," Mallory said as they walked back toward the motorcycle. "Do you think the hostess overheard us asking about Claire?"

"I don't think so. She looked pretty busy." But he wouldn't put it past a guy like Salvatore to bug the place. Something he should have considered sooner.

He put on his helmet and straddled the bike, waiting for Mallory to climb on behind him. She wrapped her arms around his waist and he vowed once again to find some other form of transportation. Being so close to Mallory was driving him crazy. He not only admired her, but genuinely liked her, far more than he should.

As he headed down the street, the front

wheel on the bike shimmied a bit. He hoped it was nothing serious—the motorcycle was their only means of transportation. Concerned, he bypassed the freeway to take side streets, trying to avoid the more congested downtown area. When he found one that was less busy, he kicked the bike into the next gear.

The handlebars jerked hard in his hands, and he realized the front tire was loose. He tightened his grip, desperate to maintain control. "Mallory, jump off before we crash."

He felt her push away at the exact moment the tire flew off, sending him airborne. He hit the pavement with enough force to rattle his teeth and had only one thought before he slipped into unconsciousness.

Mallory.

NINE

Mallory screamed as she let go of Jonah's waist to jump free. She hit the ground with a hard thud, thankfully landing on the small grassy median before rolling onto the concrete.

Pain reverberated through her body and she lay flat on her back, staring up at the star-laden sky through her helmet while struggling to breathe. This tuck-and-roll thing was getting old. She decided right then she wasn't going to do it anymore.

Unlike the night she and Jonah had jumped off the train, he didn't come rushing over to see how she was. He'd stayed on the motorcycle until the last possible minute to save her. When she could breathe, she forced herself to sit upright, sucking in a harsh breath as her muscles protested. She tested her limbs, silently acknowledging that the aches and pains weren't anything too serious. Thankfully, her new hoodie and jeans had protected her skin. She took off her helmet, the crack in the side proof that it had saved her from a far more serious injury.

"Jonah?" She swept a gaze over the area, almost missing him, as he was lying in a crumpled heap at the side of the road beneath the back end of the motorcycle. Panic stabbed deep when she realized he wasn't moving.

"Jonah!" She stumbled to her feet and rushed over. With herculean strength, she lifted the bike off and then knelt beside him. "Jonah? Can you hear me?"

He didn't move for several long seconds. Then suddenly he groaned and turned onto his back. His right arm was literally covered in blood and dirt from the road. The sight was enough to leave her feeling sick and dizzy. She quickly averted her gaze, putting a hand to her stomach.

For a moment she closed her eyes, feeling helpless. *Lord, give me the strength to help Jonah.* She took several deep breaths and opened her eyes. The nausea had receded to a manageable level. Feeling more secure in her ability to help, she loosened the strap of his helmet and wiggled it off. She pulled open her purse in order to search for her cell phone.

"Mallory?" His hoarse whisper caused an overwhelming rush of relief.

"Are you hurt?" she asked, trying not to look at his bloody arm. His injuries were likely far beyond her capabilities. Her fingers closed around the small cell phone. "Stay right where you are—I'll call 9-1-1."

"No. Don't. I'm fine." Despite his assurance, he winced and groaned when she helped him to sit up. "Just give me a minute."

"Hey, are you two okay?" A middle-aged bald guy, as round as he was tall, had opened his front door to call out to them. "Don't worry, I've called 9-1-1!"

Jonah sighed heavily. "It's okay," he called out. "We're fine. Don't need an ambulance."

"I think it's too late for that," she muttered under her breath when the man threw them a surprised look and then stepped back to shut his door. "Besides, it's best that you get checked out by a doctor, Jonah. That arm of yours looks pretty bad." So bad, she could barely look at it.

"Not an option." The firmness was back in his tone, and despite his injuries he struggled to stand. "We need to get out of here. But we obviously can't use the bike, so we'll have to call a cab."

She helped support his weight, placing her arm around his waist so he could lean on her. "We can catch a cab, but why are you being so stubborn about going to the hospital?"

"For one thing, there's still a warrant out for your arrest. And look at the bike for a minute." He lifted his chin in the direction of the seriously crumpled motorcycle. "See how the front tire came off the frame? That didn't happen by accident."

She stared in shock. "It didn't?"

"No. There was a little shimmy once we got on, and I should have stopped right then and there to investigate. I knew the tire was going to come flying off, which is why I wanted you to jump. Someone tampered with the motorcycle on purpose because we asked questions about Claire Richmond."

She swallowed hard, not wanting to believe him. But she couldn't deny how scared that waitress had looked when they'd gone out to talk to her.

She shivered, and not because of the

cold. Was it really possible someone had just tried to kill them once again?

Jonah mentally kicked himself for not figuring out the bike had been tampered with sooner. Idiot. He should have known, or at least anticipated the possibility, especially after the way everyone at the restaurant acted so weird the minute he'd asked about Claire. Even Abby had tried to warn them.

Mallory looked scared, adding to his guilt. He put more weight on his right leg, relieved when the pain wasn't too bad. His right side had taken the brunt of the crash, but he didn't think he had any broken bones except for maybe a cracked rib—the right side of his chest felt as if it was on fire.

Thank You, Lord. Thank You for keeping us safe!

"I'll call a cab," Mallory said as she opened up her phone.

He put his hand over it, stopping her.

"Not yet. Let's walk for a while first. I want to get away from here. The last thing we need is to answer a bunch of questions when the ambulance arrives. And besides, there's a good chance the police will be sent, as well."

"What about the motorcycle? Are you just going to leave it here?"

"I don't have a choice. Help me pull it off the road." He hated discovering he was more shaken up than he thought—it took both of them working together to drag the bike up over the curb. As they started down the road, he heard the wail of sirens growing louder and louder. A sense of urgency hit hard, there wasn't a moment to waste. "Come on, Mallory, we need to step on it."

"Maybe you should go to the hospital without me," she protested, even though she picked up her pace.

If he remembered correctly, there was a small strip mall just around the next corner. He tried to ignore the pain in order to walk faster. "Salvatore seems to have a far reach, and I'm convinced he could find me at the hospital, if he really wanted to." As they reached the corner, he gave Mallory a nudge. "Take a left—we're going to head back to the main road."

She didn't argue, for which he was extremely grateful. Every breath he took caused a stabbing pain in the right side of his chest. He tried to keep his breathing shallow, but that only made him light-headed.

Finally they reached the strip mall. And just in time. The lights from the ambulance raced toward them, and he quickly pulled Mallory into a doorway for a used bookstore. He wrapped his arms around her and buried his face in her hair. Her scent instantly filled his head.

She clung to him tightly as the ambulance rushed past. Even after it was long gone, he didn't move. Holding Mallory like this felt good. Felt right. And for a brief moment he wished things could be different and that she wasn't a potential witness he had to keep safe but that the two of them were just a couple on a date rather than on the run.

Mallory shifted in his arms, and he forced himself to loosen his grip. She lifted her head to look up at him but he couldn't tear his gaze away from her mouth. Before he could talk himself out of it, he lowered his head to capture her lips in a tender kiss.

Instantly she melted against him and his brain ceased all rational thought. He lost himself in the sweetness of her kiss until the shrill sound of sirens once again filled the air.

Reluctantly, he broke it off, breathing hard and looking over Mallory's shoulder as a cop car went whizzing past. It slowed in order to turn the corner, following the path the ambulance had taken to the scene of the crash.

Just as he'd suspected. "Let's go," he murmured, disentangling himself from the embrace. As much as he'd enjoyed the kiss, he knew full well he shouldn't have done it. Cops didn't do well with relationships. And getting emotionally involved with Mallory wasn't smart. He couldn't tolerate the thought of anything happening to her. If he wasn't careful, dividing his attention between her and finding the proof they needed just might get her killed.

They'd already had far too many close calls.

She stared at him for a second, as if she wanted to say something, but she simply turned away. Was she looking for an apology? He couldn't blame her if she was.

"Hey, there's a taxi," he said, catching sight of one slowing to a stop at the red light. "Come on, let's snag it."

Mallory surprised him when she put two fingers in her mouth and whistled loudly. He couldn't help grinning as she hurried ahead to catch the driver before he took off, leaving him to follow more slowly, holding his arm tight against his chest to minimize the pain.

It wasn't until they were both in the backseat that he allowed himself to relax.

They were safe for now. But they still didn't have any proof that Caruso was involved with anything illegal. And while it seemed Bernardo Salvatore was probably involved as well, chances were slim anyone would come forward to help them.

At this point, it was looking as if that proof they needed to clear Mallory might not exist.

Mallory huddled next to Jonah's warmth, trying to keep her teeth from chattering. Shock was beginning to sink in.

She wanted to go back to the brief moment when Jonah had held her in his arms and kissed her. She hadn't wanted to let him go.

But of course they couldn't just stand in the doorway of a used bookstore forever.

His kiss had surprised her but she told herself not to read too much into it. No doubt it had been a delayed reaction from surviving the motorcycle crash or just a tactic to divert attention. Besides, if Jonah knew the truth about her past, he'd likely run as fast as he could in the opposite direction.

She closed her eyes, wishing she could be the type of woman Jonah could love. But he deserved someone pure. Someone good. Someone like her sister, Alyssa. Not a fallen woman like her. Getting a tattoo under her collarbone wasn't the worst she'd done.

When the taxi driver pulled up to their hotel, she rummaged in her purse for the cash to pay the fare. It was telling that

Jonah barely noticed, and she tried to hide her growing concern as she helped him from the back of the vehicle. He leaned against her, as if his strength was waning.

She opened her room door and flipped on lights as she helped Jonah to his room. He sank onto the edge of the bed, holding the right side of his chest. "I wish you'd go to the E.R.," she murmured. His right arm was still covered in blood and grit.

"I'm fine. Probably just a cracked rib. I'll feel better after I rest a bit."

A cracked rib? Her heart sank. She sighed, knowing there was no way to avoid the task at hand. She'd need to clean up his bloody arm. "I'll be right back with some water. Stay put."

"I think I can manage that."

She took the plastic ice bucket into the bathroom and filled it with hot water. After tucking several washcloths and towels under her arm, she picked up the bucket and headed back to Jonah.

Hoping the spaghetti and meatballs she'd eaten for dinner stayed in her stomach where they belonged, she dunked the first washcloth in the warm water and glanced up at Jonah. "This is going to hurt," she warned before gently placing the soft cloth over his bloody arm. Covering the blood helped minimize her nausea but when it came time to remove the cloth, her stomach lurched.

He held himself completely still as she worked on cleaning the blood and gravel from his wound. She imagined he was in pain and couldn't bear to look into his eyes.

She doggedly kept at her task, emptying the ice bucket when the water became too red. As she worked, she grew relieved to discover the wound wasn't as bad as it had originally seemed.

She lightly wrapped his arm with gauze, and once the open areas were covered, she began to relax. She risked a glance at Jonah, disconcerted to see he was staring at her. "Almost finished," she murmured.

"Not bad for someone who claims she can't stand the sight of blood."

"Yeah, well, I think I'm starting to get used to it," she responded drily. "But that doesn't mean I want to keep bandaging you up like this. So let's not make this a habit, hmm?"

"Mallory." The sound of his husky voice saying her name made her shiver. Her hands stilled when he reached up to cup her face with his broad hand, his thumb lightly caressing her cheek. "I think you've been absolutely amazing through all of this."

She wanted to laugh and cry at the same time. He thought she was amazing? That was only because he didn't know the real Mallory Roth. She needed to tell him but the words strangled in her throat.

A smile tugged at the corner of his mouth. "Never thought I'd see the day when you were speechless."

She wanted to protest when he let his hand drop to his side. Finally, she found her voice. "Trust me, Jonah. I'm nothing special. I'm only doing what I have to."

His smile vanished and he looked almost angry. "Why do you keep doing that?" he demanded. When she stared at him blankly, he continued, "Every time I say something nice, you put yourself down. And there's no reason for it. You're a smart, beautiful, compassionate woman and whichever lowlife boyfriend told you otherwise needs his head examined."

His pop-psychological assessment was too close to the truth for comfort. She tore her gaze from his to concentrate on wrapping his arm. "Did it ever occur to you, Jonah, that you really don't know anything about me?"

"I know you, Mallory. I feel like I

know the real you, not the person you've always pretended to be."

Avoiding his gaze, she rose to her feet and went back to the bathroom to empty the bucket. She wasn't used to people—men in particular—looking past the facade she presented to the world. Most men were satisfied with having her act as an arm decoration and nothing more. "I'll get some ibuprofen. I think you're going to need it."

She wasn't running away from him, she told herself as she rummaged through her things for the medication. She just wasn't comfortable with him being nice to her, that's all.

"Thanks," he murmured, as he took the pills she held out for him. He tossed them back and swallowed them dry.

"Yell out if you need anything, okay?" she said as she turned and walked back to her room.

"Only if you promise to stop putting

yourself down," he said. "Otherwise I'll suffer in silence."

"Is that supposed to be a threat?" she asked, smiling in spite of herself. "Because if so, you could use more practice."

"Good night, Mallory."

"'Night, Jonah."

After everything that had happened, she would have thought she'd fall asleep the moment her head hit the pillow. But she kept hearing Jonah's words over and over in her head.

Did he really think she was smart, beautiful and compassionate?

Did he really know the true Mallory?

Why did that thought scare her more than anything else that had happened since she'd met Jonah Stewart?

Mallory spent a restless night, and she didn't even have cracked ribs to blame for her lack of sleep. As soon as the sun was up, she dragged herself out of bed.

After a quick shower, she felt a little more human.

There was no sound coming from Jonah's room, so she decided to let him sleep while she went in search of some breakfast.

The motel lobby had a continental breakfast set out, so she helped herself to a bowl of Cheerios and half a bagel with cream cheese. A family of four left the room, leaving behind a newspaper, and she went over to their table, planning to read while she ate.

But the main headline splashed in big letters across the front page stopped her cold.

Woman's Body Pulled from Lake Michigan.

Overwhelmed with dread, she quickly read the article, fully expecting that the victim was Claire Richmond. But she was wrong. She had to read the sentence twice before the words could sink in.

The victim was identified as Abigail Del Grato, a young waitress who worked at Salvatore's. They were still waiting for the ME to determine cause of death, but there was bruising around her neck, indicating she may have been strangled.

Mallory let out a low sound, covering her face with her hands as she remembered the stark fear in Abby's eyes when they'd spoken about Claire.

Her stomach heaved, and she had to take several deep breaths. That poor frightened girl was dead. Because of them. The young waitress had died only because she'd talked to her and Jonah about Claire. She hadn't told them anything specific, but her killer hadn't known that.

Mallory wasn't sure just how much more of this she could take.

TEN

Jonah eased out of the bathroom, using the wall for support. His effort at showering was pretty useless as the physical exertion already had sweat beading on his brow. At least he'd managed to dress himself. Raising his arms up to pull a T-shirt over his head had almost made him pass out from pain. Too bad they were running low on cash or he'd ask Mallory to pick up some shirts that buttoned down the front.

He made his way across the room, feeling disgustingly weak. His open wound had started bleeding again. He kept forgetting to take the antibiotics and he was afraid infection may have already set in.

Gingerly, he lowered himself into a chair, holding his breath when pain shot through his chest. He couldn't figure out which hurt worse, having surgery or having a cracked rib.

At the moment, he would have said they were dead even.

"Jonah?" He glanced up in surprise when Mallory came barging through their connecting doors.

The alarm on her face made him jump back to his feet, ignoring the stabbing pain. "What's wrong? What happened?"

"She's dead. Abby's dead!" She thrust the newspaper at him. "We killed her, Jonah. She's dead because she talked to us."

Dread twisted low in his belly as he recognized the name of the waitress who'd spoken to them outside Salvatore's. He took the newspaper, sank back into the chair and read through the article.

It didn't take long to realize Mallory was right.

He knew in his gut Abby'd been murdered because she had talked to them.

Knowing they hadn't forced her to talk to them didn't make him feel any better. He'd gone to Salvatore's restaurant on purpose. He'd poked the sleeping tiger with a stick, hoping for a reaction.

But he'd never anticipated something like this.

Dear Lord, forgive me. Please forgive me!

"What should we do, Jonah? Call the police?" Mallory's voice was thick with suppressed tears.

This time, he couldn't offer any comfort. Not when the acrid taste of bitterness coated his tongue. And especially not when the last time he'd held her in his arms, he'd been stupid enough to kiss her.

Feeling grim, he set the newspaper aside and scrubbed a hand over his jaw.

"I'll call Detective Butler, the guy I met with yesterday."

"Maybe we should go back to Milwaukee." A small tear escaped from the corner of her eye, rolling down the side of her face. He resisted the urge to wipe it away. "I don't care if they arrest me for killing Wasserman. I can't do this anymore, Jonah. I just can't."

He didn't want to admit she might be right about going back to Milwaukee. Abby's death proved the stakes in this game were high. Too high. He'd always known Caruso was playing for keeps, but he hadn't bargained for this. He couldn't bear knowing innocent people had already suffered as a result of their attempt to find proof against Caruso.

They needed help. Clearly, he couldn't break this case without assistance from someone within law enforcement. But he couldn't trust anyone within his district, either.

The only other contact he had was

Rafe DeSilva, his buddy in the Coast Guard who'd helped him track Jefferson's yacht after Alyssa had been captured. Since he couldn't prove drugs were involved, and the crimes weren't taking place on the water, the Coast Guard didn't have any jurisdiction. But he hoped Rafe could get him in touch with someone who worked for the FBI.

At this point, he and Mallory needed all the help they could get. And then some.

Jonah made the call to Nick Butler, but the detective didn't answer so he left a terse voice-mail message asking for a return call. He was just about to call Rafe DeSilva when Mallory returned with a Styrofoam plate heaped with food.

"Please eat something, Jonah," Mallory urged, pushing the plate of food toward him. "You look pale."

"Thanks." He wasn't that hungry, but took a few bites of bagel because he knew he'd need his strength. He dialed Rafe's number, wincing at the early-morning hour.

Rafe sounded suspicious as he answered. "Yeah?"

"Rafe, Jonah Stewart calling. I'm sorry to wake you, but I really need your help."

"Do you have any idea what time it is, amigo?" Rafe demanded in his thick accent. "And this is my day off. I'm spending well-deserved time with my family."

"I'm sorry. But I promise this won't take long. I'm in trouble. Didn't you have a friend who left the DEA to work for the FBI?"

"Yes, Logan Quail. What do you need him for?"

"I have a problem and can't go to my boss. I need the Feds."

"I don't know if Logan will be able to help you. He's been on a special task force busting up organized crime."

Perfect. Logan Quail was exactly what

he needed. His muscles relaxed as he realized he'd made the right call. "Yeah, well, organized crime is exactly why I need him. Can you give me his number?"

"Sure." Rafe rattled off the number while Jonah hastily scribbled it on motel stationery. "Is this about Hugh Jefferson by chance?"

"Yeah." He wasn't surprised Rafe connected the dots back to Jefferson. After all, they wouldn't have saved Alyssa and Gage without Rafe's help. They'd been forced to jump off the burning yacht, and Rafe's Coast Guard cutter had been there to pull them out of the water. "I'm trying to get evidence against the guy in charge of the whole money-laundering operation. Thanks, Rafe. Tell Kayla I'm sorry I disturbed you."

"No problem. Stay safe, my friend."

"I'll try." Jonah closed his cell phone and took another bite of his bagel.

"You're calling the FBI?" Mallory

asked her eyes wide. "Do you think they can help us?"

He shrugged. "I don't know for sure. The bureau likes to run things their way, and I'm not sure they'll believe your story. But it's possible this friend of Rafe's will help us off-grid."

"Off-grid? You mean unofficially?"

"Yeah. That's exactly what I mean." He stared at his phone for a minute before punching in the number Rafe had given him. He could only hope that calling Logan Quail wasn't another mistake.

Because if he put Mallory in danger one more time, he was never going to forgive himself.

Mallory wasn't sure she liked the idea of bringing more people into their investigation. Wasn't it bad enough that the one person who'd already talked to them was dead? She could remember, all too clearly, the stark fear in Caruso's ex-wife's eyes when they'd met at

Crabapple Park. Too late now to undo any damage her impromptu request for a meeting might have done. She could only hope that Rachel Camille Simon and her son, Joey, would be safe.

The thought of anything happening to them made her feel sick to her stomach.

"Logan?" Jonah said into the phone. "Rafe DeSilva gave me your number. I need help bringing down the top guy in Jefferson's money-laundering scheme, but I don't want this information to go through the Fed's normal channels, at least not yet."

There was a pause while Jonah listened to the FBI agent. She leaned forward, trying to hear what was being said but she couldn't distinguish much except for the hint of a Southern drawl. Was it possible this Logan guy wasn't even close to them? For all they knew, he was down in Texas somewhere.

"I'm glad you're familiar with the Jefferson condo project. I also have some additional information you might find interesting but I don't want to go into everything now. I'm out here on my own and I need you to promise you won't bring the rest of your team into this until we have the proof we need."

There was another pause, shorter this time, giving her the impression Logan had indeed promised.

"That should work," Jonah agreed, glancing at his watch. "I'll figure out a way to get back to Milwaukee in the next four hours."

Four hours? What on earth was he talking about? She wasn't sure how they were going to get anywhere. And she doubted they had enough cash to take a taxi all the way back to Milwaukee.

The thought of going home filled her with a strange sense of dread. She hadn't been in her condo in almost a full week, yet it seemed more like a month. During those first few days at the cabin, she'd wanted nothing more than to go home. But that was then.

For some reason, she couldn't stand the idea of going back to her old job. Not that she minded her work—decorating was fun and she had an eye for color. But after everything that had happened over the past few days, she had a new perspective on life. Being an interior designer seemed so useless. A fluff job.

Truthfully, her entire life was useless. How much time had she wasted playing the role of someone she wasn't? Too much time. She was stunned to realize she wanted to do something more. Something important. But she couldn't be a nurse, like Alyssa. Or a cop, like Jonah.

Then what? She hated to admit she had no useful skills.

"Okay, thanks, Logan. See you later." Jonah snapped shut his disposable cell phone and finished off his bagel.

"You really think we can trust this

guy?" she asked, dragging her mind back to the issue at hand.

"We don't have a choice. We can't do this without help, Mallory. You said so yourself. And if you remember, it was your idea to go back to Milwaukee."

Her thoughts were contradictory. Why was she so upset about getting more help? She should be glad they had another expert on their side, a federal agent no less. After all, it wasn't as if she'd been much help. "As long as Logan doesn't arrest me, I'll be fine."

"He won't." Jonah's phone rang and he looked down at the screen to see who was calling. "Detective Butler, thanks for calling me back. I need a favor. Will you give us a ride to the closest train station? I have some information to share on your latest floater."

She couldn't hear what the detective said on the other end of the phone, but he must have agreed because Jonah nodded. "We'll be ready. Thanks." He turned toward her. "Go and pack your stuff. Butler is going to be here in thirty minutes."

She crossed over to her room. There wasn't much to pack, aside from the new clothing she'd purchased. Since she had extra time, she went through her purse, cleaning out the junk she'd accumulated.

Way down at the bottom, she discovered a bracelet Caruso had given her in the first couple weeks of dating. She hadn't even remembered keeping it. She stared at the square-cut rubies and diamonds with distaste and seriously considered tossing the gaudy thing into the wastebasket.

But Abby's words from last night echoed in her mind. *She planned to go to the police with what she knew, and then cash in the expensive jewelry he'd bought her so she could start over someplace new.* Had Caruso given Claire jewelry the way he'd given Mallory this ruby-and-diamond bracelet?

"Mallory?" Jonah called from his room. "Are you ready?"

She dropped the bracelet back inside her purse, tugged its strap over her shoulder and picked up her bag. At the last minute, she added the Bible to her bag. "Yes. I'm ready."

There'd be plenty of time to get rid of the bracelet later. Besides, she thought, it was probably best not to leave anything too personal behind in the motel room anyway.

Jonah's coplike instincts were rubbing off on her. And so was his faith. She hadn't told him, but the few prayers she'd said had seemed to work so far. Maybe she was crazy for starting to believe, but she'd decided he was right when he'd told her believing in God couldn't hurt.

She murmured another quick prayer as she went out to join Jonah.

She didn't say much as Detective Butler drove them to the train station. She listened as Jonah explained what had happened the night before.

"Abby Del Grato actually said Claire was gone and wasn't coming back?" Detective Butler asked incredulously. "And that Claire was planning to go to the police with what she knew?"

Jonah nodded. "Yeah, but she didn't give us anything more. I'm convinced the reason she was killed was because someone caught her talking to us."

"Too bad she didn't come forward when we interviewed her along with the other employees." Butler sighed heavily before glancing at Jonah with suspicion. "And how did you know Claire used to work as a waitress at Salvatore's anyway? I didn't tell you that."

"It was a lucky guess on my part, but why didn't you tell me?" Jonah countered.

"I didn't even think about it." When Jonah didn't say anything, Butler shot him an exasperated glance. "Come on, you don't seriously think I withheld pertinent information on purpose?"

Mallory held her breath as the tension between the two of them rose to a palpable level. Maybe Jonah shouldn't have trusted the Chicago detective.

"I don't know what to think," Jonah finally muttered. "We spoke briefly to Abby outside the restaurant. And then our motorcycle was tampered with, causing us to crash. And we know Salvatore is a strong financial supporter of Caruso. So it just makes sense that this is all connected."

"Maybe Salvatore is the one who killed Claire, rather than Caruso," Mallory said, breaking into the conversation.

Both men swiveled around to stare at her. Detective Butler turned back to concentrate on the road, but she still had Jonah's attention. "What makes you say that?"

She shrugged. "I mean, we know

Claire was dating Caruso, because there were pictures of them together, but she also worked at Salvatore's. Who knows why she was silenced? The fact that it happened a month after she and Caruso had broken up makes me think Salvatore is more likely to be the guilty one."

"You have a good point," Jonah agreed slowly. "Either way, it's obvious the cases are connected."

She thought so, too. When the detective pulled up to the train station, she gathered her belongings and opened the door.

"Thanks for the loan," Jonah was saying as Butler slipped him some cash. "I promise I'll pay you back."

"Don't worry about it." The detective waved him off. "Consider it payment for the help you've given me on this case. I think we're going to have to take another long look at Salvatore's business dealings, see if we can connect him to any other crimes."

"I'd like to stay in touch, if that's okay." Jonah shook hands with Butler.

"I'll count on it." With one last wave, the detective climbed back in his car and drove away.

Mallory followed Jonah inside the downtown train station, gazing around apprehensively. She'd taken the train to Chicago before, but her senses were hyperaware as she scanned the crowd of people milling about the station. After being on the run for so long, the crush of people was unnerving.

"At least this time we get to sit on proper seats," Jonah said as they prepared to board the train.

"True," she agreed with a small smile, remembering the cargo train.

As they settled in side by side, she pulled out the Bible and prepared to read. Just sitting and staring out the window would only drive her crazy.

"You took the Bible with you?" Jonah asked in surprise.

Warily, she nodded. "Is that a problem?" Stealing a Bible wasn't exactly a good way to connect with a God she wasn't completely sure she totally believed in, she guessed.

"Relax, Mallory. It's fine. The Bibles are there for people to take. I'm just surprised that you wanted to."

She didn't want to talk about the kernel of faith she was beginning to nurture. For one thing, it made her uncomfortable to talk about God and religion. For another, they were riding public transportation, where other people could hear them.

And while she liked reading the psalms and had murmured the occasional prayer, that didn't mean she was fully converted or anything. The last thing she wanted to do was to give Jonah the wrong impression.

Especially after that kiss.

"Here, try this one," Jonah said, taking the Bible from her hands and paging to a particular spot. "It's one of my favorites."

Glancing down, she realized he'd given her Psalm 23. She'd actually read it before, but this time, the words resonated in her soul.

"'Surely goodness and mercy shall follow me, all the days of my life, and I shall dwell in the house of the Lord forever,'" Jonah read softly.

His voice was mesmerizing. "I'd like to believe that's true," she murmured.

"Believe, Mallory," he urged. "Believe in God and it will be true."

His face was close to hers, so close she could see the golden flecks circling the pupils of his eyes. She quickly averted her gaze.

Resolutely, she closed the book and put it back in her bag. "I'm a little tired. I think I'm going to rest for a while," she said.

She could feel disappointment radiating from him, but he didn't say a word.

She wanted to tell Jonah the truth about her past, but couldn't think of a way to broach the subject. Talking about her feelings was never easy, and talking about faith was even harder, so she spent the rest of the ride thinking about Psalm 23 as she feigned sleep.

When the conductor announced the stop near the Milwaukee airport, Jonah nudged her. "Time to go, Mallory."

She rubbed her eyes and ran her fingers through her hair. She hadn't so much as touched makeup in days and knew she probably looked terrible. When the train came to a stop, she followed Jonah down the metal steps and through the crowd at the terminal.

"Do you have any idea what this Logan guy looks like?" she asked in a hushed tone.

"Yeah, I do." Jonah took her hand in his, drawing her out of the way of people trying to get past. She did her best to ignore the frisson of awareness at his touch. "Over there, the tall dude wearing a cowboy hat, frayed jeans and boots."

She saw Logan the minute Jonah described him, mostly because he stuck out like a sore thumb. He looked as if he'd ridden his horse into town for a rodeo. "I thought FBI agents all wore suits and ties," she whispered as they made their way toward him.

"Apparently not." Jonah held out his hand as the cowboy approached. "Hi there, thanks for meeting us. I'm Jonah and this is Mallory."

"No problem."

She thought it was odd that Logan didn't offer his name.

"Let's get out of here. I have a hotel room secured right across the street."

Logan Quail had impeccable manners, opening doors for her and constantly calling her "ma'am." She wanted to tell him to stop it—"ma'am" made her feel old.

It wasn't until they were settled in a huge three- bedroom suite that Logan took off his hat, ran his fingers through his wheat-blond hair and faced them. "So, I hear you've gotten yourself in a bit of trouble."

"Yeah, you could say that." She listened as Jonah briefly summarized the events from the moment she'd run from Caruso to the latest victim being fished out of Lake Michigan. "We need proof that Caruso is dirty, but we don't have anything solid," Jonah finished. "Which is why we desperately need help."

Logan didn't say anything for a long minute. "Well, then, it's a good thing Rafe sent you in my direction. Because we already have Salvatore in our crosshairs, but we didn't know Senator Caruso might be involved. That bit of news takes the investigation to a whole new level."

Hearing Logan actually believed them

made her dizzy with relief. "I'm so glad," she said, speaking up for the first time since Jonah had told their story. "Please tell us you have a plan."

"Well, ma'am, now that you mention it, I do have a plan. But it's risky."

"I don't care," she said stubbornly, ignoring Jonah when he began to shake his head, disagreeing with whatever Logan had planned. "And I think I already know what your plan is. You want me to call Caruso to set up a meeting with him, don't you?"

"No. No way. That's not happening," Jonah interrupted hotly.

"That's one idea," Logan said as if he hadn't heard Jonah. "But there are others to consider—"

"None as good as that one," she interrupted. "Let's go with what we think has the best chance of working." She held Logan's gaze, refusing to look at Jonah. He didn't understand that she needed to do this. Needed to end this nightmare once and for all.

Even if it meant putting her own life on the line to get it done.

ELEVEN

Jonah couldn't believe Mallory was making plans with Logan as if he weren't sitting right next to them. As if he weren't the cop leading this investigation.

Enough was enough.

"Listen up!" he yelled. Pain shot through his chest and he put a hand to his cracked rib as the two of them fell silent, staring at him in stunned surprise. He lowered his voice to a normal level. "Mallory is not going to call Caruso to set up a meeting, got it? There's no point when we don't have anything against him. He's too smart to talk in front of Mallory."

Logan's piercing green eyes seemed to

look clear down into his soul. The agent might give the impression he was laid-back, but Jonah suspected his intense keen gaze didn't miss a thing.

And right now, he could tell Logan was wondering just how involved Jonah was with Mallory. An unspoken question he didn't want to answer.

Because he was already in too deep.

"If Salvatore was on your radar screen, Logan, then let's focus on him for the moment," he continued in a calmer tone. "Maybe once we have something solid against Salvatore, we can link him to Caruso."

"No," Mallory argued, the stubborn tilt to her chin all too familiar. He wanted to tear out his hair by the roots in frustration. "The last time we tried to investigate Salvatore, an innocent girl turned up dead. Caruso wants me—it makes more sense that we tap into him first."

Logan tipped back in his chair, glancing between the two of them with an amused expression on his face. "I'm not sure why y'all bothered to get in touch with me," he drawled in his exaggerated Southern accent. "Sounds like y'all got everything all figured out."

Jonah sighed and scrubbed his face with his hands, silently battling the pain in his chest. The thought of Mallory being in danger had made him forget momentarily about his cracked rib. He shouldn't have yelled, shouldn't have put up his arms. He took several slow deep breaths before speaking again. "You're right, Logan. Let's back up a minute. You mentioned Salvatore being on your radar screen. Rafe told me you're involved in a special task force investigating organized crime. Is there any way to link Salvatore to Abby's death?"

Logan dropped the chair back down on all four legs and leaned forward. "That's a good idea, Detective. I don't know what evidence they found on the girl because I've been in Chicago for the past few weeks. Only came up to Milwaukee today for a meeting with my boss."

"You're not going to call your boss, are you?" Mallory interjected in alarm.

"No, ma'am, I already gave you my word on that." For a second a flash of anger darkened the agent's eyes and Jonah realized that for all his cowboy charm, Logan wasn't a man to cross. "But as I was saying, we have a contact inside Salvatore's restaurant."

"Kate. Your contact is Kate, right?" Jonah asked.

Logan slowly nodded. "Yes, Kate Townsend. She called me last night, after the two of you left."

"Is she a cop, too? Was it Kate who convinced Abby to talk to us?" Mallory asked.

"No, ma'am," Logan said. "Kate isn't a cop yet. She's still in college studying criminal law. She contacted us when she first started working there, when she realized she'd stumbled into a haven for organized crime. We tried to convince her to quit, but she refused. She's been feeding us information ever since."

Jonah could tell Logan wasn't entirely thrilled with Kate being a source of information, but he also wasn't going to turn his back on whatever insights the young woman could gather. He remembered the pretty blonde waitress and had to admit the girl had guts. She was young—too young—to be putting her life in jeopardy like that.

"You need to get her out of there, Logan," Mallory said urgently, as if she'd read his thoughts.

"I've already made the call," Logan said slowly. "But she'd reported in for her shift tonight, so she's going to stick it out."

Jonah could see the stark fear in Mallory's eyes. "She needs to get out of there now," she urged. "She needs to walk away and never go back."

"Walking off the job in the middle of her shift would cause more suspicion," Jonah pointed out. "She's probably better off finishing."

Mallory still didn't look convinced. "But what if Bernardo Salvatore finds her after she quits?"

The flicker of fear in Logan's gaze was so brief, Jonah wondered if he'd imagined it. "Trust me, Mallory, we'll take care of Kate," Logan reassured her.

"What exactly did Kate tell you?" Jonah asked. "Did she uncover any details related to Claire's death?"

"Well, now, the waitresses don't talk about Claire much," Logan said. "And it took several months for Abby to confide in Kate at all. But when the two of you showed up last night, Abby told Kate that Claire was dead, and warned Kate not to mention the subject again unless she wanted to end up like Claire."

Disappointment stabbed deep. Jonah ground his teeth in frustration. "Is that all she said? We knew that much already."

Logan's expression turned grim. "No, that's not all. Claire's body hasn't been found yet, so we can't prove it, but according to what Abby told Kate, Claire Richmond was about three months pregnant."

"Pregnant?" Mallory stared at Logan in shock. She remembered the photos she'd found on the internet of Claire standing next to Caruso.

Jonah's expression was grim. "Pregnant? Do you really think that's true?"

Logan shrugged. "Why not? A pregnancy would be a really good reason to make sure her body doesn't show up somewhere."

"Unbelievable," Jonah muttered.

"So it's likely Caruso was the one who killed her," Mallory murmured. "The reason for the delay was because that's when he discovered she was pregnant.

Maybe she threatened to go public with the news."

"Certainly one theory," Jonah agreed. "Although if that's true, then her death may not have had anything to do with Caruso's money-laundering scheme."

"Maybe not, but murder is still murder, regardless of the motive," Logan said. "We get him on murder and we'll likely uncover proof related to his money laundering."

"But how are we going to prove it, considering we don't have a body?" Jonah asked.

"Good question. Caruso either destroyed the body somehow or buried it so deep we'll never find it," Logan pointed out.

The very thought made Mallory feel sick. She was appalled at the idea she'd gone out with a murderer. How could her instincts have led her so far astray? She was ashamed of herself, for the way she'd acted over these past ten years.

She'd made the same mistakes over and over again. Why hadn't she seen Caruso for what he was? Why had she allowed herself to get involved with him? All he'd done was make her feel humiliated and betrayed.

Now she wanted more than anything to make things right.

"Maybe we should try to get a search warrant?" Logan asked.

"On what grounds?" Jonah demanded. "Abby is dead. Kate's statement at this point is nothing but hearsay. I doubt that will be enough to convince a judge that a well-respected senator murdered a possibly pregnant woman."

Logan didn't look at all fazed by the prospect. "Search warrants have been issued for less."

"Not against a senator," Jonah argued. "We absolutely have to do this by the book."

"Which takes us back to square one," Mallory murmured. "We don't have any other options than for me to contact Caruso. Jonah, let me confront him about Claire's pregnancy. He might be surprised enough to let something slip."

"No way," Jonah said again. "I already decided against you contacting Caruso as bait."

Logan pursed his lips and stared down at the toes of his cowboy boots. "I can tell you're not going to budge on letting Mallory help," he said finally. "You obviously don't want her in any danger. So what should our next step be?"

"I think we're better off using that plan as a last resort. Hey, what about Caruso's ex-wife?" Jonah asked, completely switching the topic of conversation. "Mallory, you met with her—what will it take to convince her to work with us?"

"Ironclad protection for her and her son," she answered without hesitation.

"We can offer her witness protection," Logan said.

Mallory shook her head. "That's not going to work, Logan. She's the vice president of a successful company. Why should she give it all up to testify against Caruso? Her wealth and position of power are the only things keeping her and her son alive."

A long silence hung heavily between them.

She leaned forward. "Jonah, listen to me. Allowing me to contact Caruso is our best option. Logically, you know it, too. I understand you don't want me in danger, but you're the one who told me to have faith. Well, I'm asking you to have faith, too, Jonah. I'm asking you to have faith in me."

"I'm not agreeing to anything until we've exhausted all options," Jonah said. "I still believe there has to be another way."

He hadn't agreed, but she suspected that he would if they didn't come up with anything better.

She didn't feel an overwhelming sense of relief. Instead, her stomach churned with turmoil. She gripped her fingers together, so he wouldn't know how deathly afraid she really was.

Fear didn't make her any less determined, though. She was the one who'd blithely gone into a relationship with Caruso. It was only right that she should be the one to help bring him down once and for all.

Jonah unrolled Logan's map, racking his brain to come up with an alternative to using Mallory as bait to lure Caruso.

Okay, maybe he was too emotionally involved. So what? If it meant keeping Mallory safe, he was perfectly fine with that. This time, he didn't intend to make any mistakes. And he knew allowing Mallory to set up a meeting was a mistake.

Especially when he wasn't exactly in top physical form to keep her safe.

"My source tells me these three warehouses are abandoned," Logan said, pointing to them on the map. Jonah was irritated at the way Mallory's gaze clung to Logan as she listened intently. "The property was purchased by a company called Green Speak, with the intent of leveling the warehouses to make room for a new structure they planned to use for building wind turbines. But after the real-estate market crashed a few years ago, they put their plans on hold. We could easily get a team in place prior to the meeting between you and Caruso."

"Okay, so we need some reason for Caruso to agree to a meeting at an abandoned warehouse," Jonah said with a heavy sigh. He wasn't agreeing to Mallory being the one to set up the meeting, but hadn't yet come up with another way to get Caruso there.

Logan opened his mouth to say something but was interrupted by his cell phone. He glanced at the screen with a frown. "It's Kate," he murmured before bringing the phone up to his ear. "Hello?"

Jonah glanced warily at Mallory as they listened to Logan's one-sided conversation.

"Okay, listen, we'll be there in an hour."

"What's going on?" Jonah demanded.

"Guess who's having dinner at Salvatore's tonight?" Logan's eyes gleamed with anticipation.

"Caruso?" Jonah couldn't believe their luck.

"Yes, with Salvatore himself. But not until eight o'clock."

"I don't want Kate anywhere near them," Mallory said forcefully.

Jonah knew Mallory was traumatized by Abby's murder and put a reassuring hand on her arm. "Kate has been working at the restaurant for several months, Mallory. There's no reason for Salvatore to suspect her at this point."

"Let's go." Logan's attitude was all business now. "We can discuss the best plan of action on the way down to Chicago."

Jonah nodded and they headed down to the main level, to Logan's vehicle.

He couldn't help feeling thankful that the ridiculous idea of using Mallory as bait to draw out Caruso had been put on hold.

As far as he was concerned, the plan would stay on hold, indefinitely.

Mallory didn't have much to add to the conversation between Jonah and Logan about listening devices and other gadgets that might be of some use to overhear the conversation between Salvatore and Caruso.

She wrapped her arms around her waist to keep from shivering. The summer-evening air was actually very nice but she couldn't seem to shake the feeling of impending doom.

When they arrived in Chicago, Logan pulled into the parking lot of a fancy hotel. He flashed his ID and the parking attendant waived him through. "You're staying here?" she asked incredulously.

Logan nodded. "Yeah, it's all part of my cover story. I own several oil wells in Texas, which means I have to live the part of being wealthy."

"You didn't mention you've been working undercover," Jonah accused. "Have you already met with Salvatore? Do you actually have business meetings with him?"

"We've met, but no, I haven't had any business meetings with him." Logan's tone held a note of exasperation. "We've been on this task force for months, but it's slow and painstaking work to build a case like this."

"Sorry," Jonah muttered. "I know better than anyone how tedious law-enforcement investigations can be."

Logan parked his Jeep in the underground parking lot and then went around to the back and opened the door. Curious, Mallory followed, surprised to discover the rear of his vehicle looked as if he had robbed an electronics store.

"You're not really thinking of bugging Salvatore's table, are you?" Jonah asked.

"Do you have a better idea?" Logan drawled.

The burgers they'd eaten along the way sat like a rock in Mallory's stomach. "Sounds risky," she said. "If they suspect Kate, she'll end up dead, like Abby."

"We'll talk about this inside," Jonah said, as Logan put several electronic items into a small duffel bag before tossing it over his shoulder and slamming the car door shut.

None of them spoke as they made their way up to Logan's room. Once inside, Logan set the duffel bag on the table and opened it up. "Salvatore always sweeps the restaurant for bugs before he comes in to eat, so we only have a couple options. We can wire Kate, but it's not likely they would say anything incriminating in front of her so I'm not in favor of that option."

"You can bug the table, but Kate would have to do that once they're already seated," Jonah said, catching on to Logan's train of thought.

"Exactly. It's more risky, but we have the best technology Uncle Sam has to offer." Logan opened a container the size of a ring holder and revealed a small black disk that was slightly thicker than a dime yet a bit smaller in circumference. "Kate can place this right under the table and remove it as soon as they're finished eating, with no one being the wiser."

"Great idea," Jonah said with renewed enthusiasm.

Mallory wasn't so sure. "Seems too easy," she said with concern. "Have you already tried this? You know it'll work?"

"We've used it once before and it worked beautifully," Logan assured her, closing the box with a snap. "There's no reason to think it won't work again."

Mallory didn't bother to hide the doubt on her face. "Except for the fact that Abby was killed late last night simply because she spoke to us."

"Mallory, it's very possible that there were other things that happened late last night that caused Abby's death," Jonah pointed out. "We don't know for sure that it's only because she spoke to us."

"Trust me, I'm not going to let anything happen to Kate Townsend," Logan said firmly. "We're going to do this tonight, and tomorrow, my team is going to relocate Kate someplace safe."

Mallory sighed, knowing there was no way to talk either of the men out of this. Both of them were convinced they couldn't fail. She wished she had the same certainty.

Helplessly, she closed her eyes. *Dear Lord, please keep Kate Townsend safe in Your care.*

Jonah knew Mallory was distressed over their plan to bug Salvatore's table, but while he understood her apprehension, he also felt a deep sense of anticipation.

This plan of Logan's could work. And if they managed to get some sort of incriminating evidence against Caruso tonight, this entire mess would be over soon. And Mallory would be completely safe at last. He didn't like thinking about how his priority had changed from simply closing the case to clearing Mallory.

Jonah took the earpiece Logan held out to him and the small ring box containing the black disk to the other side of the room. He opened the box and then spoke in low tones but Jonah could hear every word plain as day.

"Amazing," he said in admiration. "When are you going to get in touch with Kate?"

"We're going to hand over the disk outside the restaurant while she's on break," Logan said, glancing at his watch. "Which should be in about fifteen minutes."

Considering it was already seven-fifteen, the timeline was a tight one. "And where are we going to sit and listen?"

"We're going to stay in the Jeep right where it's parked," Logan said. "The restaurant is only half a block away."

"Won't the concrete walls interfere with the signal?" Jonah asked.

"The signal was clear last time I parked on that same level, but we'll test it again to be sure." Logan took the disk out of the ring box and put it in a small, clear plastic sheath that was no bigger than a nickel. "Here, you take these two sets of earpieces and go sit in my Jeep.

I'll take this out to the restaurant and you can let me know if you don't hear anything."

"How do we let you know?" Mallory asked.

"Text me." Logan settled the cowboy hat on his head and flashed a grin. "I'm going to bump into Kate and make a big deal out of apologizing as I hand her the disk."

"Sounds good." Jonah waited a few minutes after Logan left before he led the way down to the parking structure. Once they were seated in the backseat safely behind Logan's tinted windows, he showed Mallory how to put the earpiece in.

Amazingly, they could hear the traffic noise on the street, as Logan walked down to Salvatore's. "Testing," he drawled in a low tone.

"It's so clear," Mallory whispered.

"Yeah." Jonah couldn't help being impressed. He quickly texted Logan to let him know the listening device worked fine.

It was getting close to Kate's break time, and he wished he could see Logan as well as hear him. The minutes ticked by slowly. Then he heard a muffled gasp, and Logan's deep drawl came through crystal clear. "My apologies, ma'am, I didn't mean to step on your foot."

"Well, maybe you should watch where you're walking, big guy," a young female voice said with sharp annoyance.

"Yes, ma'am. I guess I'm used to wide-open spaces like we have in Texas, not the crush of people here."

"Whatever." Kate's annoyance radiated through the listening device. "I have to get back to work."

There was no more talking, only the sound of traffic and people's voices in the background. Apparently Logan didn't head back to the parking garage right away because it took time for him to return. Jonah figured he must have walked around the block before returning to the hotel.

Logan finally slid into the Jeep. "We're all set. Nothing more to do except wait."

Jonah knew from long experience that waiting was the hardest part of a stakeout. Kate must have had the device in her pocket because they could hear the sounds of dishes being stacked and menu items being discussed. Then they heard Kate's voice.

"Mr. Salvatore, how nice to see you again. We were expecting you at eight."

"Our meeting ended early. Do you have our table ready?"

"Yes, sir, right this way."

"I'd like my bodyguard to check out the place first," they heard Salvatore say.

"Of course, sir. Excuse me for a moment while I let the chef know you've arrived earlier than planned."

Jonah glanced at Logan. "She's pretty

good, knew enough to get out of the way of the bodyguard sweeping for bugs."

"No, Kate, don't go." Salvatore's sharp tone came through the earpiece. "I'd like you to stay."

There was a long pause before they heard Kate's voice. "Yes, sir."

"Logan, do something," Mallory whispered tersely. "Kate's in trouble!"

Logan's expression turned grim, and Jonah understood. There wasn't anything they could do now except wait for this to play out, hoping and praying Kate wouldn't get caught.

TWELVE

Mallory couldn't breathe. Her heart pounded so hard against her ribs that she put a hand to her chest to ease the ache. She couldn't bear knowing that, any minute, the bug they'd handed to Kate would be found.

"All set now?" Kate's voice asked politely.

"Yes." Salvatore's tone was curt and they could hear the sounds of the two men settling into their seats. "Send the wine steward down to bring us the usual."

"Right away, sir."

Mallory momentarily closed her eyes with relief. Kate was safe. At least for now. She reached over and grasped Logan's elbow. "How is it possible that Salvatore didn't find the bug?"

"The disk I gave Kate uses a completely different frequency than the normal listening devices," Logan explained.

"You knew she'd be safe," Mallory said, feeling foolish for being so worried.

Logan's grin faded. "No, ma'am. I hoped she'd be safe, but I couldn't know for sure. Salvatore has deep pockets and I had no way of knowing if he'd upgraded his technology, too."

Slightly mollified she sat back in her seat, listening to the background noises that were coming through her earpiece. "Sounds like Kate is still in the kitchen," she murmured.

Logan nodded. "She can't place the bug until she takes their order for dinner without raising suspicion."

"How does she know to do all this?" Mallory asked as her stomach once again knotted with anxiety.

Logan's expression turned grim. "Apparently, she has a knack for undercover work," he muttered.

She hid a smile. It was clear Logan had a soft spot for the young waitress and didn't like using Kate's talents even though she obviously was good at her chosen career.

Too bad she didn't have the same skill set. Mallory's stomach was so upset she feared she'd end up with a bleeding ulcer if she had to do what Kate was doing.

Mallory strained to listen, although with all the background noises it wasn't easy. The minutes dragged by slowly, until finally they heard Kate addressing the restaurant owner. "Are you ready to order, Mr. Salvatore?" she asked.

The two men took their time ordering their food. When she heard Caruso's voice ordering the Chilean sea bass—his distinct northern nasal tone a direct contrast to Salvatore's deeper voice carrying a hint of his Sicilian heritage—she shivered.

The man was cold. He'd murdered at least one person and attempted to murder her, yet he still sat leisurely eating an expensive dinner as if he didn't have a care in the world.

"I'll have the chef prepare your food right away, Mr. Salvatore," she heard Kate say.

Again there was no response from either man, as if it were beneath them to respond personally to the hired help. But when they began to talk in low voices, she realized Kate had succeeded in placing the disk beneath their table.

"Have you found her yet?" Salvatore asked.

"No. She has help, which has made her much more difficult to find," Caruso answered with annoyance.

Mallory experienced a surge of satisfaction when she realized the two men were discussing her. She was fiercely glad that, with Jonah's help, they'd managed to elude Caruso.

"I'm not pleased at how you've managed to drag me into your mess for the second time, Tony." The implied threat underlying Salvatore's tone was unmistakable. "To have them show up here is inexcusable. I will not tolerate incompetence."

"Don't threaten me. I've helped make you a rich man, Bernardo."

"And you wouldn't be in office without me."

"I know, I know. Don't worry. I'll take care of my loose ends the same way you've taken care of yours."

Jonah glanced back at her, and she knew he was thinking about Abby's body floating in Lake Michigan. But while the two men obviously were discussing their various crimes, they were careful enough not to say anything blatantly incriminating.

A wave of helplessness washed over

her. What if this was all for nothing? What if the two men didn't give them anything to work with?

"Your soup, Mr. Salvatore and Senator Caruso," Kate said. Mallory had the impression Kate mentioned both names on purpose. "I hope you enjoy your meal."

"Where is the ground pepper?" Salvatore asked sharply. "Is this the service you provide? I expect better, or this will be the last meal you serve."

"Yes, sir," Kate murmured in apology.

There was a long silence as the men ate their food. The next bit of conversation centered on the restaurant business. It wasn't until the two men had been served the main course that their conversation turned back to important matters.

"Tell me, Tony, what is the next step in solving your small problem?"

"I told you not to worry. I have a contact inside the MPD helping me track them down."

Mallory gasped. Jonah was right—his boss really was helping Caruso.

"And is that all?" Salvatore asked softly. "You're just going to sit back and wait for someone else to find her for you?"

"What do you expect?" Caruso asked with clear annoyance. "I have to be back in Washington by the middle of next week for the Senate vote on the budget bill. I can't ignore the obligations of my career, Bernardo."

"Perhaps it's time to use her sister as leverage."

Mallory reached out to grab Jonah's arm. "We have to do something to keep Alyssa safe!" she hissed in a low tone.

"Drummond is with her constantly. She's never alone," Caruso said. "And besides, the Feds are watching them. I'm not about to walk into a trap."

The Feds? Really? Mallory relaxed back in her seat.

"Idiot," Salvatore mumbled beneath

his breath. "Tony, have you forgotten how to bluff? If your ex-girlfriend is on the run, she won't know that her sister is safe."

"You have a point, Bernardo."

Mallory could easily imagine how Caruso's mind was exploring the possibilities. And despite knowing the Feds were watching over Alyssa, she couldn't help but worry.

"I have a couple other options, too," Caruso continued. "But rest assured I will have everything taken care of before I leave for Washington. Including hiding all evidence so that it doesn't wash ashore to be discovered quickly."

The subtle dig did not go unnoticed.

"Watch yourself, Anthony," Salvatore said in a soft yet dangerous tone. "Your public position is extremely vulnerable, while I have the support of the family behind me."

There was a tense silence and Mallory

imagined they were glaring at each other as they exchanged their veiled threats.

"Bernardo, you worry too much. I will have everything taken care of. I managed to eliminate the earlier threat, didn't I?"

"After you were stupid enough to get her pregnant."

"Because she lied to me." Caruso was clearly backpedaling, trying to make amends. "And I learned from my mistake. Our goals are still the same, Bernardo. We both want to be rich. Trust me to make that happen."

There was another pause. "All right, then, I will grant your request for five days," Salvatore said. "But I expect results by next Wednesday, understood?"

"Of course."

Within a few minutes, Kate returned. "Are you both finished, Mr. Salvatore?" she asked.

"Obviously," he replied in a snide tone. Mallory could hear dishes being stacked, and then suddenly, there was a loud yell followed by the sound of dishes breaking.

"You imbecile!" Salvatore shouted. "Clean up this mess!"

"Yes, sir. I'm so sorry sir!" Kate's voice was full of horror. "I'll clean it up right away, sir!"

"You're fired!" Salvatore shouted. "Get this woman out of my sight!"

"Right away, Mr. Salvatore."

"I'm sorry. I'm sorry," Kate sobbed. Once again, the sounds of voices in the background along with dishes clanking together made it apparent that Kate had retrieved the bug from under the table and put it back into her pocket. They could hear someone telling Kate to put her stuff together and get out.

Logan ripped the earpiece out of his ear, jammed the key into the ignition and started the SUV.

"Where are we going?" Mallory asked, barely having time to buckle her seat belt before he barreled out of the parking garage.

"To pick her up," Logan replied tersely. "She must have set that whole scene up so that she'd get fired."

Mallory's jaw dropped in surprise. "She did? You mean that wasn't part of the original plan?"

"No," Logan spat the word with annoyance as he cranked the steering wheel with more force than was necessary before turning onto the street. "That wasn't part of the plan."

Mallory grinned. She was looking forward to meeting this Kate, who obviously had a thing or two to teach her.

Jonah glanced down at the notes he'd taken. He felt good knowing that their suspicions had been confirmed, yet he was just as disappointed that the two men hadn't said anything more damaging than veiled innuendos.

He glanced up as Logan drove well be-

yond the restaurant, miraculously finding a place to park. Logan slammed out
of the car, muttering that he'd be right
back.

Jonah exited the passenger seat, opening the back-right passenger door to
slide in next to Mallory. Within a few
minutes, Logan and Kate returned, obviously arguing.

"You should have followed the plan,"
Logan said.

Kate tossed her blond hair. "My way
was better." She turned in her seat,
holding out her hand. "Hi, I'm Kate
Townsend."

"Jonah Stewart, and this is Mallory
Roth," Jonah said, making quick intro-
ductions as Logan pulled back into traffic. He shook her hand, as did Mallory.
"Thanks for your help back there."

"No problem." The gleam in Kate's
eyes gave him the impression she had
enjoyed every moment.

"I told you this isn't a game," Logan

snapped. "You're lucky all he did was fire you."

Kate rolled her eyes and then turned back in her seat so she could buckle her seat belt. "Don't be such a worrywart."

Jonah hid a grin as Mallory choked back a laugh. Despite the seriousness of the situation, the relief of knowing they'd pulled off their mission was enough to give them a rush of adrenaline.

"So you're Anthony's ex-girlfriend?" Kate asked, glancing back at Mallory as Logan made his way to the interstate. There was no doubt he was planning to take Kate to Milwaukee, far from Salvatore.

"Unfortunately." Mallory scowled and Jonah knew she regretted the decisions she'd made. "And you're the detective wannabe."

Kate laughed. "Yep, that's me. Actually, I graduate at the end of the semester, so my career is well within reach. And it's also why I'm not packing up to leave town the way the cowboy keeps demanding."

"I told you, we'll make arrangements to transfer your college credits to another institution," Logan said, inserting himself in the conversation.

"But I'll lose a semester if I do that," Kate argued.

"How long have you worked for Salvatore's?" Jonah asked, hoping to sidetrack the argument brewing between Logan and Kate.

"Just over a year." Kate let out a heavy sigh. "Too bad I had to quit—I made good money working there."

"How did you figure out Salvatore was involved with organized crime?" Mallory asked.

"They didn't exactly keep it a huge secret," Kate said. "Honestly, if I'd have known, I wouldn't have applied for a job there in the first place. But my roommate was working there and gave me a good reference."

"They must not have known you were studying criminal law," he said, "or there's no way they would have hired you."

"I'm pretty sure they assumed I knew what was going on there because of Angela, my roommate. Salvatore is her uncle on her mother's side. Angela is studying business but she's made it clear she plans to get a job with her uncle when she graduates." Kate wrinkled her nose. "Talk about keeping business within the family."

"You took a huge risk tonight," Jonah pointed out. He understood why Logan was so frustrated with Kate. Even now, she was acting as if this was nothing more than a game, when in fact it was anything but. Salvatore and Caruso played for keeps.

"I didn't have much choice, once I knew what was going on in there." Kate shrugged off his praise. She turned to sit back in her seat. "Did you get anything useful from them?" she asked Logan.

"They confirmed our suspicions but didn't give us any new information," Logan admitted.

Jonah leaned forward. "Is it true the bureau is watching over Alyssa and Gage?" he asked.

Logan lifted a shoulder. "I'll check to be sure, but I wouldn't be surprised. To be honest, I think they might have been waiting to see if Mallory would show up."

Mallory reached over to tightly grip Jonah's hand. "Please check right away, Logan. I need to know Alyssa's safe."

"She'll be fine," Jonah murmured, helpless to defuse the tension radiating from her. "Gage won't let anything happen to her."

"I know, but he's not a cop and he can't possibly sit with her 24/7, either." Mallory worried her lower lip between her teeth, and he wished he had the right to draw her into his arms, hold her close and kiss her.

"Don't panic until we know what we're dealing with," Jonah reassured her. "Caruso isn't going to make a move toward Alyssa until he's exhausted a couple other options first."

"I hope you're right, Jonah." Mallory's wobbly voice betrayed her fear. "I really hope you're right."

The trip back to Milwaukee seemed to take forever. It was late by the time they all trooped back up to the large three-bedroom suite Logan had obtained for them.

"Kate, I'd be happy if you shared my room," Mallory said, indicating the large bedroom containing two queen-size beds along with its own private bathroom. "That way we'll have some privacy from these guys."

Kate quickly nodded. "Sounds great. Thanks."

The two women disappeared into the bedroom, closing the door behind them.

Jonah glanced at Logan. "I don't like the deadline Caruso created for himself. I'm afraid he might make a play for Alyssa to bring Mallory out of hiding."

"I hear you. Let me make a couple calls tonight, but it could be that we won't hear anything until tomorrow," Logan said.

"I understand. But I think we should strike first. And I have an idea."

"Let's hear it," Logan drawled.

Jonah shook his head. He needed some time to think through the details. "No, make your calls first. It's late—we'll have plenty of time tomorrow to talk it through."

Logan nodded and went to make his phone calls.

Jonah went to his room and closed the door, going over the steps in his mind. There had to be a way to make his idea work. Because he refused to put Mallory in the center of danger.

He cared about her far too much.

* * *

Mallory awoke early and glanced over at Kate, who was still asleep. They'd been sharing the room for two days now, and she was reminded of the early days when she and Alyssa had shared a room while growing up.

She missed her twin so much. And she was determined to do whatever was necessary to keep Alyssa out of this.

Her stomach grumbled as she showered and dressed, making her remember she hadn't been able to eat much of the meal they'd ordered from room service last night. The four of them had spent the entire day considering various plans but had not been able to come to an agreement.

Of course, Logan had wasted almost half the day trying to convince Kate to go into witness protection, to no avail. Mallory had admired Kate's ability to stick to her guns, and selfishly, she'd wanted Kate to stay.

She eased open her door, silently entering the main living area of the suite. The other two doors were closed, so she knew she was the first one up.

In the small kitchen area, she made a pot of coffee and nibbled on some of the leftovers from the night before. But her stomach cramped and she gave up pretending to eat.

She glanced down at the map Logan had left on the table as she sipped her coffee. There were some drawings on it but she didn't understand exactly what the scribbles meant. The guys had stayed up late, trying to decide what their next steps would be.

When Jonah's bedroom door opened, she was so startled her hand jerked, spilling coffee on the table.

She jumped up to get a napkin to clean up the mess. "You scared me."

"I'm sorry," he murmured.

She took a deep breath, trying to slow her racing heart. She didn't know why her nerves were on edge; it wasn't as if they'd agreed to implement anything today. But at the same time, time was running short. They had to do something, and quick. "Would you like some coffee?"

"Uh, no thanks. I'm going to church."

She blinked in surprise and frowned. "Church? It's Sunday?" How could it be Sunday already?

He smiled. "Yes, it's Sunday. There's a small church down the road that offers an early service. Let everyone know I'll be back in a couple hours."

Mallory couldn't remember the last time she'd attended church, mostly because she'd never wanted to. But as Jonah walked toward the door, she jumped up. "Do you mind if I come with you?"

He froze, and for a moment she thought maybe he was looking for time alone, but when he turned to face her, there was no denying the pleased surprise on his face. "I'd like that. It's about a mile away, though, and I was planning to walk. Is that all right with you?"

A walk sounded perfect. Better, really, than sitting through a church service. "I don't mind at all." She glanced down at her casual attire. "I don't have anything else to wear," she said by way of apology.

"Under the circumstances, I don't think God is going to mind," he murmured.

His comment made her smile and relax. Her preconceived notions about God and church were obviously a bit outdated.

"Are you ready?"

As they walked outside into the cool summer air, she lifted her face, enjoying the breeze and her surroundings. The sky was a prettier shade of blue than she'd seen before and the white puffy clouds were the kind little kids would see as animal shapes. Being outside without fearing for her life was a novelty. For the first time in what seemed like forever, she felt like a normal person. As if she and Jonah were the only two people on the earth.

The church was picturesque—brown brick on the outside with a tall steeple and beautiful stained-glass windows. It wasn't elaborate but it was beautiful in its simplicity. Funny how she'd never considered a church to be noteworthy before now.

As Jonah approached the steps leading up to the front door, she hesitated, gripped by a sudden surge of panic. She fought the urge to turn and run all the way back to the relative safety of the hotel room.

Going inside to attend church services was a big step for her. A step made even more important because she was going with Jonah.

She slowly realized that becoming closer to God would impact her relationship with Jonah.

Irrevocably changing her life—forever.

THIRTEEN

Mallory kept her head down as she entered the church, feeling like a fraud. She avoided eye contact with the other parishioners as she slid into the pew beside Jonah.

The early-morning service didn't have a strong showing, but there were more people than she'd expected in attendance. The members of the choir didn't seem to mind—they sang the opening hymn with gusto and the rest of the church members quickly joined in.

Including Jonah.

His deep baritone was soothing and helped Mallory relax. If she had a decent voice she might have joined in, but she was content to read the words in an attempt to follow along. She shouldn't have been surprised that Jonah knew every word of the song—after all, attending church wasn't a foreign event to him the way it was to her.

Church music wasn't normally her thing but she had to admit the song was more upbeat than she'd expected. Jonah belonged with the rest of the choir, she thought with a flash of pride—his voice was absolutely amazing. She was surprisingly disappointed when the last verse of the song ended. When he kept his hymnal in his hands, rather than putting it back into the holder, she followed suit, holding on to hers, too.

As the pastor started his sermon, Mallory thought she'd be bored out of her mind, expecting the usual fire-and-brimstone type of preaching she'd seen in movies. No doubt she'd hear about the perils of being a sinner, a situation she was all too familiar with. But surprisingly, her attention was snagged, almost immediately, by the pastor's viewpoint on the topic of forgiveness. She had the uncanny feeling he was speaking directly to her. And when he quoted from the Bible, the words resonated deep within her.

"'Therefore, my friends, I want you to know that through Jesus the forgiveness of sins is proclaimed to you. Through him everyone who believes is set free from every sin, a justification you were not able to obtain under the Law of Moses. Take care that what the prophets have said does not happen to you.'"

For a moment Mallory sat in stunned silence, thinking about her own sins and whether or not God would really forgive them. Jonah had told her all along that God would forgive her, but hearing the words from him was one thing. Hearing them from the pastor was something different. She hadn't been sure she could really, truly believe.

Until now.

When Jonah reached down to pick up the hymnal that had dropped from her nerveless fingers, she gave him a tight smile. "Thanks," she whispered.

His brows were furrowed with concern. "Are you all right?" he asked in a hushed tone.

She swallowed hard, amazed at his perceptiveness. She nodded and glanced away. How could she explain her feelings? Jonah had told her about his partner's death—had bared his soul—but she'd never confided her own deepest shame.

Yet maybe this was God's way of telling her the time had come to do just that.

Jonah could feel how tense Mallory was beside him, and he prayed for strength and understanding so he might help her with whatever burden she carried.

When the church service ended, Mallory didn't get up to leave like the rest of the parishioners. He sensed she wanted to talk but maybe didn't know how to start.

"Mallory, why don't you tell me what's bothering you?" he asked gently. "I could tell the pastor's sermon meant something to you but I'm not sure I understand. Why is it that you think you don't deserve forgiveness?"

"Because deep down, I've always thought he was right," she confided. "That what happened was really all my fault."

His breath froze in his chest as he digested her words. Was she saying what he thought she was saying? "Who was right, Mallory? What do you mean?"

She toyed with the strap of her purse for several long seconds. "Garrett Mason, the quarterback and captain of our high-school football team." Her voice was so low he had to strain to hear what she was saying. "During our senior year of high school, I had a huge crush on him, but he didn't know I existed. One Friday night, I asked Alyssa if we could switch identities. I wanted to work her shift at the Burger Barn, because the team was planning to go there after the game."

Jonah's gut knotted with anger as he slowly began to understand where her story was going.

"I shamelessly flirted with Garrett, making it clear I wanted to go out with him. I even told him my real name and the joke I'd played on the manager, pretending to be Alyssa. He laughed and told me I obviously like to live dangerously. I blithely agreed. When he offered to wait for me after the end of my shift, I was ecstatic. My plan had worked."

She paused and as much as he didn't want to hear the details, he knew she needed to tell him. To let go once and for all. "Then what happened?" he forced himself to ask.

"He drove me back out to the high-school stadium so we could sit under the bleachers. I was thrilled, especially when he kissed me, but then—" Her voice trailed off.

Red-hot anger surged, momentarily blinding him. It took all the control he possessed to keep his feelings from showing. The last thing he wanted to do was to scare her. "Whatever happened wasn't your fault, Mallory. No matter what he said, he's the one who broke the law, not you."

"Logically I understand that. I knew what the term *date rape* meant. But when I remember how I acted back then, I can't deny my actions started the chain of events. And I have to own up to them. I'm the one who switched places with Alyssa, just so I could see him and talk to him. I'm the one who flirted with him. Maybe I did give him the wrong impression, but I didn't mean to."

"I know, Mallory. I know. It's his fault, not yours."

She shook her head as if still unable to believe that. "Afterward, I was—shattered."

He could only imagine what she must have gone through. He placed his arm around her and hugged her close, wishing he could go back and change the past. No woman should have to suffer like she had. His heart ached for her lost innocence. "I'm sorry, Mallory. I'm so sorry," he murmured.

"I didn't tell anyone, except Alyssa." Her voice was muffled against his chest. "She tried to convince me to go to the police, but I couldn't. I was afraid everyone would believe what Garrett said, that I asked for it."

"You didn't," Jonah repeated, fighting to keep the rage from his tone.

"That's when I signed up for Tae Kwon Do. And as I became stronger, I grew angry and bitter. I turned my back on God. I also decided that I'd never let any man get the upper hand, that relationships would be on my terms. That I'd never let myself get emotionally involved." She shifted in her seat and looked up at him with tearful eyes. "Except I ended up doing the same thing all over again, by dating Caruso. Maybe he didn't assault me like Garrett did, but he wants to do something worse."

"You couldn't possibly know Caruso was involved in criminal activity," Jonah protested, brushing away a damp strand of hair from her cheek. "Cut yourself a little slack, Mallory. Everyone makes mistakes."

She let out a harsh laugh. "Not the kind of mistakes I've made. And besides, that's not the worst of it." Now that she'd started talking, it seemed as if she couldn't stop. "Listening to the pastor today, I finally believed God would really forgive my sins. Except as we were saying the Lord's Prayer at the end of the service, I realized it wasn't good enough. I have to forgive Garrett for what he did to me, don't I? Not only Garrett, but Anthony, too." There was a long pause before she whispered in a low, agonized tone, "Honestly, I'm not sure I can do that, Jonah."

He didn't know what to say because he wasn't so sure he could forgive the two men, either, even though he knew he should. God expected him to forgive them and anyone else who trespassed against him.

He pulled her close and held her for a long time, offering what meager comfort he could. And he wondered humbly if God had sent him Mallory, not just so that he could help her believe, but so that she could help him become a better Christian.

"Your note said you were attending church, but you were gone so long, we were starting to worry something had happened to you," Logan drawled, his eyes glittering with a pent-up anger that wasn't reflected in his laconic tone.

"Why didn't you invite me?" Kate asked from where she sat curled up on the sofa.

"Sorry," Mallory murmured. Jonah hoped the two of them wouldn't notice Mallory's reddened and puffy eyes. "We stayed longer than we anticipated."

"I take full responsibility," Jonah quickly interjected. "We talked for a while afterward. I should have called to let you know we were on our way."

"Next time, I'd like to go with you," Kate said.

Logan lifted his eyebrows as he glanced at Kate, as if surprised to know she'd have wanted to go along, but he didn't say anything other than, "I ordered breakfast if y'all are hungry."

Jonah glanced over at the array of breakfast items Logan had ordered from room service, in quantities that would support a small army, realizing his appetite had returned. He glanced at Mallory, relieved to see she appeared anxious to eat something, too.

Neither of them had said much on the walk back, mostly because he couldn't think of a way to tell her how much he admired her strength. He took solace in the knowledge that Mallory looked better, as if finally telling him the truth had given her some peace.

Knowing what he did now, he understood Mallory's actions better than ever. All along, he'd suspected that she'd hidden her real self from the world behind a facade, but now he knew for certain.

He somewhat understood the choices she'd made and knew she'd learned from her mistakes. And most of all, he was thankful she'd come into his life when she had.

Dangerous thoughts, he warned himself as he headed over to the table Logan had cleared for their meal. He could admire Mallory from afar, but he'd already crossed the line once by kissing her. He couldn't allow a lapse like that to happen again.

He was a cop and would always be a cop. He knew, better than anyone, the type of stress his career had on families.

But he was glad when she took a seat next to him at the table, leaving Kate to sit beside Logan. Jonah bowed his head and asked for God's blessing, thanking Him for the food they had to eat and for keeping them safe from harm. The way Mallory and Kate both murmured, "Amen," warmed his heart.

Logan didn't add to the prayer, but he waited for Jonah to finish before digging in. There were several long moments of silence as everyone concentrated on eating. Jonah was tempted to tease Logan about the way he dug into his food, as if he had a stomach the size of Texas. But he refrained, since he was doing his part in putting a large dent in the meal.

When Logan finished, he pushed back

from the table, picked up a mug of coffee and eyed Jonah over the rim. "Do you want the good news? Or the bad news?"

Mallory froze at his words, her fork halfway to her mouth. The quick flash of fear in her eyes seared his soul.

"Don't play games, Logan." Jonah knew he was overreacting, but after everything Mallory revealed less than an hour ago, he wasn't in the mood for Logan's teasing.

"The good news is that I heard from one of the guys on my task force. He confirmed Alyssa and Gage do have FBI agents keeping an eye on them. The bad news is that the two agents are probably going to be pulled off by tomorrow. Apparently they're convinced Mallory isn't going to return, as that would put her sister in danger."

"No!" Mallory jumped to her feet. "They can't leave them alone. Caruso will find them!"

Jonah's heart went out to Mallory. "Take it easy. We're not going to let that happen. Remember, we still have twenty-four hours before they're in any danger."

"Jonah's right, but we need to decide on a plan and move forward today," Logan said. "Kate knows the names of two guys who are for sure working for Salvatore."

"James Kiefer and Kevin Graves," Kate said. "They both come in a lot to talk to Salvatore when he's there."

Jonah's eyes brightened. It was exactly the opening he'd been looking for. "Then let's use them to lure Caruso to the warehouse. I'll place a call to Caruso pretending to be one of Salvatore's men, claiming I caught Mallory sniffing around Salvatore's restaurant, and say I'm holding her at one of the abandoned warehouses."

"Except he knows you and Mallory

were at the restaurant together. It's why he killed Abby," Logan argued.

"But maybe he'll believe I went back later and saw something I shouldn't have," Mallory agreed slowly. "I think we can make this work."

Logan scowled. "But that was forty-eight hours ago. Why would the guy wait?"

"Maybe we could make Caruso believe I escaped and he just got me back," Mallory said, her eyes betraying her inner fear.

Jonah reached out to take Mallory's hand. "Don't worry. We can make this work without putting you in any danger."

He turned toward Logan. "We need backup if we're actually going to trap Caruso."

It was Logan's turn to be silent. "Well, now, I'm not so sure about that idea," he drawled.

Jonah's gaze narrowed suspiciously. "Why not?"

"Because Salvatore himself is the main target of the FBI task force, which means my boss isn't going to go along with this plan, especially if there's any possibility it will risk our chance to nail Salvatore." When Jonah kept glaring at him, he added, "You asked for this to be kept off-grid, and I agreed. I knew all along that helping you and Mallory trap Caruso would ultimately blow my cover, putting my career in jeopardy. Rafe is a good friend, and you sounded like you were in trouble, so I decided to take the risk."

Mallory pushed away from the table and began stacking up the dirty dishes, hoping neither Jonah nor Logan would notice her shaking hands. She'd thought for sure Logan's plan would work.

But now she was plagued with doubt. And fear.

"You told me you have a team," Jonah insisted hotly, not bothering to hide his anger.

"I have some guys who will help us off-grid," Logan insisted. "I told you I had backup."

Jonah still looked tense, as if he wasn't reassured. "You're sure these guys are trustworthy? It's not just our lives, but Mallory's and Kate's on the line."

"You don't have to remind me," Logan said testily. He let out a heavy sigh. "I don't know them that well," he finally admitted.

"I need you to be sure, Logan. I've already been betrayed by one of my fellow officers."

"What do you want me to say, Jonah? Do you want me to call this whole idea off?"

"No," Mallory said sharply, whirling around to face them. "We're not going to call this off. We need to do this. We can't risk placing more innocent people in danger."

For a moment Jonah's gaze held hers, and she was shocked at the agony reflected there. He was worried about her. Truly worried.

"She's right, Stewart," Logan said. "We don't have time to waste. If we're going to do this, we need to agree on a plan and get the ball rolling, ASAP."

"I'll be your backup," Kate offered.

"You're not a cop!" Logan shouted, his face red with anger.

"Kate and I will be fine together," Mallory spoke up. "Kate knows how to use a gun. Let's just finish this, okay? We'll be fine." She refused to consider any other option.

Ironic how she hadn't trusted a man to get close to her over all these years, but now she was putting her very life into these two men's hands.

"Let's go down to the SUV and pull the equipment we'll need," Logan suggested. "We'll need to plant listening devices in the warehouse."

"I'm going to call Alyssa while you're getting the equipment," she said to Jonah. "She needs to know what's going on."

He nodded and the three of them left the hotel room. She quickly dialed Gage's number, and luckily, she finally got through to him.

"How is Alyssa?" she asked. "Did the surgery go okay? Is she feeling better?"

"Yes, she's fine." Gage's voice changed subtly. "Is Jonah there? I'd like to talk to him."

"Why? Did something happen?"

"Nothing you need to worry about. Just have him call me."

She tried not to take it personally that Gage didn't trust her enough to pass on the message. "No problem. I'll have him give you a call."

"Okay," Gage said, although his tone

clearly indicated he wasn't thrilled with the delay. "Hold on while I get Alyssa."

"Mallory?" Tears filled her eyes when she heard her twin's voice. "Are you really okay?"

She blinked the tears away with an effort. "Yes, but listen to me, Alyssa. You and Gage need to be careful. I just found out that the FBI has been watching you both, waiting for me or Caruso to show up. But starting tomorrow, they're not going to be watching you anymore. I want you and Gage to go someplace safe, understand?"

"Yes, I understand." Alyssa's tone seemed to grow stronger knowing there was a potential threat. "I'll let Gage know."

"I'm sorry, Alyssa." Mallory wished more than anything that she could be with her sister. "We're going to try and finish this once and for all, but I don't want you to wait. Get out now, okay?"

"We will. But, Mallory, you need to

stay safe, too. What has Jonah gotten you into? He promised me he'd keep you safe."

"He's determined to protect me. He's the one going into danger, not me. Just take care of yourself, okay?" Mallory closed her eyes, wishing she could tell Alyssa everything. How she'd gone to church and opened up to Jonah. That he hadn't run away from her, even after hearing the truth. That he'd held her hand as they'd walked back to the hotel. That she had fallen for him.

But this wasn't the time. "I love you, Lyssa," she said instead.

"I love you too, Mal," Alyssa replied. "Call me every day, okay? I want to know you're safe."

Mallory swallowed against the hard lump in her throat. "I will. Take care, Alyssa."

"You too, Mal," her twin murmured, her voice fading. The pain meds must have caught up with her.

Mallory closed her phone and spent a few minutes pulling herself together. She had to be strong. She could face anything if it meant keeping her sister safe.

She opened Logan's laptop computer, and on an impulse, she did another search on Claire Richmond.

The same photographs and articles came up as before, only this time, she examined the pictures more closely, trying to see if there was any evidence of Claire's pregnancy.

But there was no betraying bump in the woman's slim figure. Based on the timeline, she figured Claire was only about twelve-to-fourteen weeks along. Was Claire's pregnancy the reason she thought her modeling career wouldn't last? No wonder she hadn't totally given up her waitressing job at Salvatore's.

Her gaze rested on a familiar bracelet circling Claire's wrist. Her stomach knotted as she zoomed in to get a better look.

The picture was grainy, but there was no mistaking the square shape of the emerald-cut rubies and diamonds. She blinked and ran over to dig through her purse for the bracelet, hoping she wasn't mistaken.

She wasn't. She held the bracelet Caruso had given her next to the photograph and realized it appeared to be the same piece of jewelry. Caruso had claimed it was a one-of-a-kind piece. She'd believed him, as the designer's initials were engraved on the back of the clasp.

Seeing the same bracelet around Claire's wrist seemed too much of a coincidence.

Hadn't Abby said that Claire was going to sell an expensive piece of jewelry to start over? Was this bracelet the item she was going to sell? The two girls had talked the night before Claire had disappeared.

If this bracelet was the exact same one he'd given to Claire then didn't the bracelet prove that he'd seen Claire the night before she'd disappeared?

She imagined the struggle as Caruso tried to kill Claire. Had the bracelet fallen off? Or had he taken it? Either way, he must have gotten the bracelet back, either right before or right after he'd killed her.

She stared at the bracelet, suppressing a shiver of distaste. How horrible to think she had worn the same bracelet as a murdered woman. Did Caruso plan to give it to his next girlfriend, after he'd killed her?

They had to stop him before that happened. All they needed was a way to prove her theory.

FOURTEEN

Mallory quickly saved the photo of Claire wearing the bracelet onto Logan's hard drive. Was it possible there were other photos of Claire wearing the bracelet after she and Anthony had broken up? She tried several other general searches without success.

What she needed was some photos of Claire with her friends. Curiously, she logged on to Facebook, just to see if Claire had ever had a presence there. She discovered there were a lot of Claire Richmonds listed, but eventually she found a Claire Richmond in Chicago whose photo looked familiar.

When she clicked on the photo, she discovered Claire had a page that her family and friends must have created as a way to honor her memory. Several had posted heartfelt messages saying how much they missed Claire, and others begged Claire to come home.

For a moment, Mallory was overwhelmed with sadness. Seeing the photos of the young, smiling blonde only emphasized the loss. Deep down, she knew Abby had been right. The pretty girl wasn't coming home ever again.

She painstakingly went through all the photos where Claire was tagged. Unfortunately, most of them were head shots, so there was no chance of even seeing a bracelet.

But then she found one where Claire was dressed up in a cocktail dress, standing beside another woman at what appeared to be a fancy restaurant. Her heart leaped into her throat when she could make out the same bracelet around Claire's wrist. But when was the photo taken? There was a date listed as to when the photo was uploaded, but that didn't necessarily mean the photo was taken at the same time.

The uploaded date was just five days before Claire's disappearance. She sat back, her mind whirling with possibilities. There had to be some way to track down when the photo was taken. Did either Jonah or Logan have ways of finding the woman in the photo with Claire? She wasn't tagged, so she must not be on Facebook.

If they could find a way to prove the date of the photograph, they would have something they needed to implicate Caruso in Claire's disappearance. And maybe, just maybe, that would be enough for the authorities to believe her side of the story over Caruso's.

She picked up the bracelet again and carefully put it in a zippered compartment of her purse for safekeeping as she anxiously waited for Jonah, Kate and Logan to return.

* * *

"Get the door, will you?" Jonah said, balancing the box of electronics in his arms.

Kate obliged, as Logan was also carrying a similar box.

"You're back!" Mallory exclaimed, leaping off the sofa. "Come here and look at what I found," she said, gesturing toward the computer screen.

He and Logan set their boxes on the floor and then crossed over to the coffee table where she had the laptop set up. He immediately recognized the photo of Claire Richmond. He frowned. "I don't think it's big news that Claire had a Facebook page."

"See this bracelet here around her right wrist?" Mallory said, pointing at the screen. "That's the same bracelet Caruso gave me on our third date."

Logan's head jerked up at that comment. He was standing on the opposite side of the computer and leaned over to get a better look. "Well, now, are you sure about that?"

Mallory pulled the bracelet out of her purse and set it on the table next to the computer. Logan whistled in surprise but Jonah could only stare at the bracelet in shock. As Mallory explained how she saw the same bracelet on another photo of Claire standing next to Caruso, he could barely contain his excitement.

"It's possible Caruso took it back from Claire and gave it to me," Mallory was saying. "He claimed it was a one-of-a-kind item. If we could nail the timeline as to when this photo was taken, we might be able to prove that Caruso saw Claire shortly before her disappearance."

"Unbelievable," Jonah murmured. Leave it to Mallory to find the clue they needed. He wanted to leap up and pump his fist in the air. "This is it, Mallory. We can easily use the bracelet itself as a way to get Caruso's attention."

"I don't understand," she said.

He glanced at Logan. "What if we changed the plan a bit? We can call my boss, who we know is working for Caruso. We can let him know we have this bracelet to set up a meeting. Once we have Finley, we'll use him to get to Caruso."

Logan grimaced and nodded. "I see what you're saying, but remember, the bracelet is only circumstantial evidence at this point. It's not a murder weapon or DNA found at the scene of a crime. It also might not even be the same bracelet." Logan shrugged. "Mallory is still the key witness who overheard him covering up a murder."

"Yeah, but don't you see that this way is safer? Finley doesn't know why I cut off all communication with him. He has no way of knowing I suspect him of being dirty. I'll let him know I want to discuss the bracelet as evidence and provide Mallory's testimony. He'll be anxious to get his hands on both the bracelet and Mallory—he won't be able to say no."

Deep in his gut, Jonah knew this was the way to go. It was the only way to keep Mallory away from Caruso.

"I don't know if I like that idea," Mallory said slowly. "To be honest, I'd rather face Caruso than your boss. What if Finley arrests me despite what you tell him? Caruso could easily find a way to have me killed in jail."

"Don't worry, Mallory. I wouldn't actually turn you in. This would just be a way to get to Finley." The more he thought about his plan, the better he liked it. Finley deserved to be used as bait to get to Caruso. And Mallory would be totally safe.

"And what if Finley isn't the dirty cop, but someone above him is?" Logan asked.

"Finley is the only one I've been talking to since we discovered Crane was dirty. He reports directly to the chief of police. I find it difficult to believe the chief is involved in this."

Logan was silent for a long minute. "Your decision," he said grudgingly. "If you want to try that route then count me in."

"Me, too," Kate added, earning another scowl from Logan.

He felt light-headed with relief. All along, he'd been so worried he'd fail Mallory, the same way he'd failed Drew. He'd tried not to become emotionally involved, but he knew he was. He cared about Mallory, far more than he should.

As much as he wanted to, he knew he couldn't pursue his feelings. She might see him in a positive light now, but how long before the extended hours of his job and the horrible things he saw every day wore on their relationship? He couldn't bear to see the same look in Mallory's eyes that he'd seen in Cheryl's, right before she'd walked out on him.

He knew his feelings were for real,

but he understood that Mallory was dependent on him for safety. She was embracing her faith, but that didn't mean she cared about him, specifically.

He shook off his uncertain thoughts. Time enough to worry about the future later. Right now, they needed to plan out the next step. For the first time in the past twenty-four hours, Jonah felt good about the direction their investigation was going. He knew they were finally on the right track.

And he firmly believed God was guiding them.

Mallory wasn't sure she agreed with Jonah's plan, but she couldn't deny she was glad they were doing something. Glancing at the clock, she was surprised to realize it was only an hour since she'd spoken to Alyssa.

According to Jonah, Gage had already taken Alyssa someplace safe, which was a relief.

"Call your boss and set up the meeting in this warehouse here," Logan said, pointing to the map. She leaned closer to see it was the one located farthest to the east. "We'll have our surveillance cameras and bugs set up well before he can get there."

"All right." Jonah took a deep breath and pulled out his cell.

"He's not going to answer on Sunday," Kate said.

"His office phone sends messages to his cell phone," Jonah explained. He turned his attention to the phone call. "Lieutenant Finley, this is Jonah. I have something important we can use against Caruso. Meet me at the warehouse on Fourth and Harper tonight—I don't want to come in because I'm being followed. Call me back as soon as you can." He quickly rattled off the new number.

Jonah snapped his phone shut and looked at Logan. "The trap has been set."

"Guess we should head down to the warehouse, then." Logan settled his cowboy hat on his head as he started toward the door. "Kate and Mallory can wait for us here."

She opened her mouth to protest, but surprisingly, Jonah beat her to it.

"The women are coming with us, Logan. We need to stick together."

Logan narrowed his eyes and crossed his arms over his chest as he glared at Jonah. "Why expose them to danger?"

"We stick together," Jonah repeated. "When I was helping Gage stake out Hugh Jefferson's yacht, we left Alyssa back in the motel alone to keep her safe, except she was anything but. We didn't realize Crane had found her until we saw him leading her to the yacht at gunpoint. I'm not going to make that same mistake. We all go together."

Mallory hadn't known that detail. She crossed over to place a hand on Jonah's arm. "Thanks, Jonah."

"Three against one," Kate piped up cheerfully, apparently not the least bit fazed by the deep scowl creasing Logan's brow. "We outnumber you, Logan."

Logan lifted his hat long enough to swipe a hand over his hair before settling it low on his brow as he glared at Jonah. "Fine, we'll do this your way. But I still think bringing them along is a bad idea."

"Your objection is so noted," Kate said smartly, and Mallory coughed to hide a grin.

The four of them left the hotel suite and headed down the stairs to the main lobby. As they walked outside, Jonah wrapped a protective arm around her waist.

She smiled up at him, wishing she could tell him how she felt. Opening up to him after church had lightened her heart and soul more than she could have imagined. And while she was still working on the forgiveness angle, at least as far as Garrett and Caruso were concerned, she was amazed that Jonah didn't seem to hold her past against her.

Of course, his being nice to her could be nothing more than friendly consideration for what she'd gone through. It didn't mean he cared about her on a personal level.

Except there had been that kiss.

She and Kate slid into the backseat, leaving Jonah and Logan up front.

"Earlier, you mentioned Alyssa and Gage. Who are they?" Kate asked.

"Alyssa is my twin sister, and Gage is her boyfriend." Thinking about her sister made her smile. "Although I guess they could be engaged by now."

"Wouldn't surprise me," Jonah muttered.

"You have a sister? Is she your identical twin?" When Mallory nodded, Kate grinned. "Did the two of you ever switch identities to fool people?"

Mallory's smile faded but amazingly,

her stomach didn't cramp painfully at the mention of that night, the way it used to. Because of Jonah. And her newfound faith in God. "Not very often, no."

Kate seemed oblivious to the subtle change in mood. "I would have loved to have a sister and especially a twin. But I only had brothers. Three older brothers, all in various types of law enforcement."

"Figures," Logan said drily. "And I bet you drove them crazy."

Kate laughed. "Not hardly. They were the ones who tortured me, not the other way around."

"There's the warehouse," Jonah said, bringing an abrupt end to the light-hearted conversation.

"I see it." Logan didn't stop but kept driving. Both men were peering intently through the windshield. Mallory did the same, craning her neck to check out the area surrounding the warehouses. The one they were looking at using had two separate garage doors in the front covered with graffiti. There was only one streetlamp out front, providing just enough light for her to see that all three buildings looked pretty dilapidated. She couldn't imagine why they hadn't been leveled a long time ago.

"They look abandoned," Jonah murmured.

"Looks can be deceiving," Logan grimly pointed out. "Let's hope they're not currently being used as gang hangouts."

"Maybe we should go around the block, just to be sure," Kate spoke up from the backseat.

From Mallory's angle in the back, she could see Logan's jaw tighten with annoyance, but he obliged Kate's request, making a big circle so that they saw the warehouse from different angles.

"There's a narrow driveway between the two warehouses there, leading around to the back," Jonah said. "If we park there, the car will be tucked out of sight from the street and away from the streetlight."

"Exactly what I was thinking," Logan said, making a left turn into the narrow driveway. He pulled around so that the building completely blocked the view of the SUV from the road. He put the vehicle in Park but kept the engine running as he turned around in his seat to look at her and Kate. "I'd like you two to wait here for a minute, at least until we verify the place is empty."

"No way," Kate said, trying to open her door. But it was locked, because Logan hadn't turned off the SUV.

"I'm in agreement with Logan on this one," Jonah said. "We just need five minutes to make sure the place is empty."

Mallory nodded, putting her trust and faith in Jonah. "All right."

Kate threw up her hands in disgust. "Okay, five minutes. But I'm going to be ready to drive away if they're not."

The two men climbed out of the vehicle. They stopped at a door on the side of the building and tested the handle, but it must have been locked, so they headed for the front. Mallory watched them until they disappeared from view. Time passed with excruciating slowness.

When Jonah tapped on her passenger window a few minutes later, she jumped from surprise, her heart leaping into her throat. Kate bailed out of the car and Mallory followed more slowly, admiring the younger girl's apparent nerves of steel.

Clearly, a career in law enforcement wasn't in her own future.

"Are you okay?" Jonah murmured, as they walked around to the rear of the vehicle.

"Of course." She'd rather be here than waiting at the hotel, but she couldn't totally hide her nervousness.

Jonah opened the back of the Jeep. "The place is empty, so our plan is to plant a few of these bugs."

"We can help," Kate offered.

"Take this inside to Logan," Jonah said as he thrust the small box into Kate's hands. He tucked the last box under his arm rather than giving it to Mallory.

"I'm not helpless. I can help, too," Mallory said testily.

Granted, Kate was studying criminal law, but she wasn't a cop any more than Mallory was. Yet the men seemed to treat Kate as more of an equal.

"You've helped us a lot already," Jonah said. "Finding the bracelet in photos of Claire Richmond was pure genius."

She hadn't been looking for a pat on the back so she dropped the subject and followed Jonah inside the warehouse through the open garage door. The interior was dark thanks to the grime coating the windows, and she glanced around, wondering where the light switches might be located.

Next to a tall stack of crates, Kate and Logan were crouched over the box of supplies, going through the contents. Jonah was on the other side of the building, setting crates up to use as a make-shift ladder, so she began examining the walls for a light switch. She finally found one, right near the side door.

Just as she was about to flip the switch, Jonah shouted, "Wait! Everyone freeze!"

"What's wrong?" Logan demanded.

Afraid to move, Mallory slowly turned her head to look over at Jonah.

"We need to get out of here," Jonah said grimly. "This place is wired to blow."

FIFTEEN

Mallory quickly dropped her hand from the light switch. What if the switch was the dynamite trigger? A chill spiraled down her spine. She could have easily killed them all.

"Are you sure?" Logan demanded as he rose to his feet. He held out a hand to help Kate up but she ignored it, crossing her arms over her chest.

"Yeah. I'm sure." Jonah slowly backed away from the pile of crates. "But if you want to see for yourself, go ahead."

"It's possible the owners were planning to blow these up in order to build their new wind-turbine plant," Kate said, as if trying to find a logical reason for what Jonah had found.

"I don't think so." Jonah's expression was grim. "Demolishing existing buildings with explosives is a detailed and precise process, with small amounts of dynamite placed in strategic locations." Jonah was continuing to back up slowly until he stood in the center of the room. "I'm not an expert, but from what I can tell, there's enough dynamite here to blow up the entire neighborhood. Far more than would be needed to bring down three abandoned warehouses."

Everyone fell silent for a moment as the implication of Jonah's assessment sank in. Logan was scowling deeply, and Mallory knew he was probably feeling guilty for suggesting they use these warehouses for a meeting in the first place.

"Well, if it isn't Detective Stewart. You arrived earlier than I expected."

At the sound of a strange voice, Mallory shrank back against the wall near the side door. From where she stood, she could just barely make out the tall figure standing in the open area where they'd left the garage door open.

"Chief Ramsey? What are you doing here?" Jonah asked, trying to hide his surprise.

"Meeting you, of course." Dread curled through her stomach as the chief of police stepped forward, his weapon leveled dead center on Jonah's chest. She glanced at the side door, wondering if she'd have time to slip through and escape before anyone noticed. "Lieutenant Finley was kind enough to let me know you'd contacted him. Keep your hands where I can see them, or I won't hesitate to shoot."

Both Logan and Jonah went still at his words, and Mallory understood why. Was it possible the police chief didn't know the building was wired to explode? Apparently not, as he'd surely realize one gunshot would be enough to ignite the dynamite.

Unless he was trying to bluff? Either way, they couldn't take a chance on any weapons being fired.

From the corner of her eye, Mallory could see that Kate had melted backward, disappearing behind a small stack of crates. And just in time, as Ramsey narrowed his gaze as he glanced at Logan. "Who are you?"

Mallory watched Logan turn his body so that he was facing Ramsey while helping to cover Kate's hiding place. Jonah mirrored Logan's move, trying to block Ramsey's view of her. Taking the bit of coverage he provided, she moved closer to the door, relieved to feel the handle pressing into the small of her back.

"Special Agent Logan Quail with the FBI," Logan replied in his deepest Southern drawl. "But I can't say it's a pleasure to meet you, sir. Why don't you put the gun away so we can talk this out? I'm sure we can reach a mutually acceptable agreement."

While Logan was speaking, she silently flipped the lock open and turned the handle. Thinking of Kate hiding behind the crates gave her a surge of grim satisfaction. The four of them against one chief—there should be no reason they couldn't find a way out of this.

"FBI?" Ramsey echoed in shock. "I don't believe you. You're bluffing."

"No, he's not bluffing," Jonah said.

"Keep your hands up!" the police chief shouted, when it looked as if Logan was reaching for his pocket.

She chose that moment to open the door a crack and slip through, using the darkness as a cover. Thankfully, clouds covered the moon. She quickly and silently closed the door behind her and then stood for several long seconds, her heart pounding in her chest as she waited to be discovered.

When nothing happened, she wanted to collapse with relief. But instead, she forced herself into action. She needed to call for help. She grabbed her phone and inched along the wall toward the back side of the warehouse where they'd left Logan's SUV. She couldn't call 9-1-1 so she quickly texted Gage.

The minute she turned the corner, she gasped when strong hands gripped her shoulders painfully. Horrified, she looked up into Anthony Caruso's leering face.

"Gotcha," he said with a cold, empty smile.

Jonah faced the chief of police. He knew Mallory had just slipped out and he was worried about what she might find out there. He had to move this along and go after her. "It's time to give up, Chief. It's over. We have the evidence we need against Caruso. I'm sure if you cooperate the D.A.'s office will go easier on you."

Ramsey took a step back, keeping both men easily within firing range. "I don't think so," he said. "All I have to do is kill both of you and I'm off the hook. I've worked hard to hype up the gang killings in the area, so it won't be a stretch for me to ensure your deaths are attributed to gang warfare. Especially since you've been so accommodating, coming down here to an abandoned warehouse. This will play out perfectly in the media."

Jonah realized he'd made a huge mistake. He'd automatically suspected Finley rather than thinking about the possibility that the dirty cop could be someone higher up the chain. He'd told Finley to meet them at the warehouse, but he should have anticipated that Finley—or in this case, Chief Ramsey—would come early, too.

His mistake that could easily get them all killed.

He couldn't believe he'd once again let his emotions get in the way of doing his job. He'd been so concerned with protecting Mallory that he'd allowed himself to be distracted from what was truly important. Solving this case.

His fault. They were standing in a warehouse full of dynamite at gunpoint because of his foolish mistake.

"You can't shoot both of us at the same time," Logan pointed out, calling Ramsey's bluff. "Is it really worth risking your life? Let's talk this through."

Jonah quickly added to what Logan was doing, trying to keep Ramsey talking. "Tell us how you got mixed up with Caruso," he invited. "If he blackmailed you into helping him, then we can probably keep you out of jail."

Ramsey shook his head. "Nice try, Stewart, but it's not going to work. Drop your weapons and get over there to stand closer to your FBI friend."

Jonah hesitated, not sure what to do. If he refused to move, Chief Ramsey might fire in an attempt to convince him to move. And that would likely set off the dynamite hidden behind the crates.

Yet moving toward Logan would mean giving up their advantage. Because no matter how good Ramsey might be with a handgun, there was no way he'd be able to shoot both of them if they were far apart.

"I said, move!" Ramsey yelled.

"Keep your voice down," a second voice said from somewhere behind Ramsey. "This might be an abandoned section of the manufacturing district but there's no sense in taking foolish chances. But you've already blown it anyway. How could you be so stupid as to let this woman escape right under your nose?"

Jonah's heart lodged in his throat when he saw Senator Caruso with his arm locked around Mallory's neck and a knife pressed against her side. He forced her to walk into the warehouse, her back arched at an awkward angle as he kept her body solidly in front of his.

Mallory's eyes were full of silent apology as she met his gaze across the room. But once again, he accepted full responsibility for this mess. He'd all but encouraged Mallory to escape. Right into Caruso's hands.

"Let her go, Caruso," he demanded angrily.

"You're not the one calling the shots here," Caruso replied. "Now tell me where the bracelet is."

Jonah fell silent, caught off guard by Caruso's demand. He was fairly certain Mallory had put it in her purse, which was likely in Jonah's SUV. But she could have just as easily left it back in their hotel suite.

"If you don't answer, I'll start cutting her up until you do," Caruso threatened. He saw Mallory wince as Caruso pressed the point of the knife harder against her side. The chilling expression in the senator's eyes convinced Jonah he wouldn't hesitate to make good on his threat.

"He doesn't know where the bracelet is," Mallory said, apparently trying to sound brave, as much as she could manage with Caruso's arm locked around her neck. "I'm the one who hid it. Let me go and I'll show you where it is."

Logan pretended to be confused by Caruso's abrupt demand. "Why do you care about a stupid bracelet?" he asked.

"Because I haven't gotten this far without being meticulous about loose ends," Caruso replied tersely. He tightened his grip around her neck, making Mallory's face grow red as she struggled to breathe. "I'm not letting you go, Mallory, so save yourself some pain and tell me where the bracelet is."

Jonah desperately wanted to rush over and yank Mallory out of harm's way. But he could only watch helplessly as Caruso used Mallory as a pawn in his deadly game.

"The bracelet..." Mallory's voice came out as little more than a croaked sound since he was holding pressure against her windpipe. Caruso obliged by loosening his arm around her throat. Mallory gulped in several breaths of fresh air. "I have it in a safe place back in our hotel room," she finally admitted. "I'll take you there."

Jonah wanted to yell out in protest. No way did he want Mallory going anywhere alone with Caruso. "I'll take you," he interjected. "I know right where she put it."

"No, you don't," Mallory argued, shooting him a glare that silently implored him to shut up and trust her. "I hid it after you left."

Jonah knew she wasn't being entirely truthful. He was equally torn between stalling for time and getting them all out of the rigged warehouse. The more Ramsey and Caruso talked, the more he was starting to believe that neither man knew the warehouse was a bomb waiting to blow.

"Forget about the bracelet," Chief Ramsey said in a curt tone. "I'll make sure my officers find it and I'll get it to you."

Caruso hesitated, as if considering the possibility. Jonah could tell Caruso didn't like letting Ramsey call the shots, especially since the bracelet was evidence that could be used against him. "I want the bracelet," he said. "And I don't believe she left it in some hotel room. Give me a couple minutes to search their vehicle, okay?"

Ramsey scowled. "Make it quick."

Jonah glanced at Logan, knowing that they were going to have to make a move, and soon. Their only hope was to distract Ramsey and Caruso enough for them to rush them head-on. A risky plan at best, with the dynamite surrounding them.

Yet it was one step above getting shot point-blank.

"You're right," Mallory suddenly said.

"I do have the bracelet with me." Her gaze was locked on his and Jonah was trying to understand what she was silently trying to tell him. Her hand was tucked inside her sweatshirt pocket— was it possible she'd managed to make a call before she was grabbed by Caruso?

He was almost afraid to hope. He tried to figure out how long they'd been standing there. It seemed like forever, but he knew it couldn't have been more than five to ten minutes.

At that moment, a tower of crates came crashing to the floor. The sound made everyone jump in surprise, including him. But when Logan headed straight for Ramsey, he realized that Kate had provided the distraction they needed.

He ran toward Caruso at the exact moment Mallory used the element of surprise to leverage Caruso's arm up just enough to duck underneath. He rammed his head into Caruso's torso, causing them both to crash to the ground. He heard Mallory cry out in pain.

Out of the corner of his eye, Jonah could see that Logan and Ramsey were wrestling for the gun. He paid dearly for allowing that brief look. Caruso hit him square in the face. He jerked backward, his head bursting with pain. For a moment darkness threatened, but he fought back against Caruso, exchanging blows, doing his best to ignore whatever was going on around him.

He hoped Mallory and Kate would run for help, but of course they didn't. He had the slim advantage of being on top, pinning Caruso to the concrete floor. But Caruso wasn't going down easily. He stretched his arm out wide, and Jonah realized the senator was reaching for the knife he must have dropped.

Jonah leaned forward, putting more pressure against the man's throat. Mallory's foot swept the knife well out of reach, sending it skittering across the room. He wanted to shout at her to get into the SUV, but he was distracted by blood.

Bright red blood.

Dripping onto the concrete floor right where Mallory was standing.

Caruso had stabbed her.

Mallory could barely tear her gaze from where Jonah and Caruso struggled on the floor. She was feeling more light-headed by the second and knew she was losing too much blood.

Please, Lord, grant Jonah the strength to get away from Caruso!

"Mallory!" Kate called from the other side of the room. Her arms and legs didn't want to work very well, as she turned toward the other woman. "Grab a piece of crate!"

In the distance Mallory could hear the wail of sirens and she hoped and prayed that help was on the way, since she'd texted Gage asking for help and giving their location. She took a piece of crate that Kate thrust in her hands, but found that she lacked the physical strength to lift the board high enough to hit Caruso.

But she noticed Kate didn't have the same problem, as she hit Chief Ramsey on the back of his head. Logan grunted as the chief collapsed and he managed to wrestle the gun away without the weapon going off.

Logan tossed the gun outside, far out of anyone's reach, before he went over to help Jonah. Mallory blinked when Kate came up beside her.

"What's wrong?" Kate asked.

She held her hand against her side. "I have to sit down," she murmured.

"You're bleeding!" Kate exclaimed. "Why didn't you say something sooner?"

She shook her head, finding it difficult to concentrate. She didn't even notice that Jonah and Logan had managed to knock out Caruso.

"Come on, we need to leave here," Jonah said, putting his arm around her for support. She clung to him, hating the fact that she didn't have an ounce of strength.

Jonah must have realized how bad off she was because suddenly he swung her into his arms. "Let's go!"

"The car is this way," Logan said, hanging back.

"The car won't help if the building blows," Jonah said, breathing heavily. "Come on!" he insisted. She felt him crane his neck back to look behind them. "Caruso's trying to get up!"

She tucked her head in the hollow of his shoulder, trying to ease the bouncing as he ran. When Logan and Kate came up beside them, she tried to get their attention. "He has cracked ribs."

"Give her to me," Logan said, understanding her concern.

Before Jonah could reply, an earsplitting boom filled the night, shaking the earth and sending all four of them airborne.

SIXTEEN

Jonah couldn't breathe—he felt as if he had a knife stabbing his heart. But he still crawled frantically on his stomach toward Mallory.

Please, Lord, keep her safe. Let her live—please.

He finally reached her, several feet from where he'd landed. She was unconscious, but he wouldn't allow himself to believe the worst. He caught her wrist, closed his eyes and concentrated on feeling for a pulse.

Finding the faint beat almost made him weep with relief. The sirens were louder now, and he had to believe they were coming for them.

"Jonah?"

Hearing Logan's voice made him raise his head and glance around. "Over here!"

Miraculously, both Logan and Kate didn't appear to be badly injured, judging by the way they rushed over to Mallory's side. "Is she okay?" Kate asked anxiously.

"She has a pulse," Jonah said, ignoring the deep stab of pain that accompanied every word. He couldn't be sure, but he thought maybe he'd broken his rib to the point that the bone was poking into his lung. "But it's fast and faint. She's lost too much blood."

"She'll be fine. Medical help is on the way," Logan assured him.

"Don't give up, Mallory," he murmured, reaching over to brush her hair off her cheek. He couldn't bear to think about losing her. "Don't give up on me—on us. Do you understand?"

Mallory stirred, and his heart raced with hope, but she didn't open her eyes.

He wished the ambulance would get here faster.

"Press this against the wound in her side," Kate said, stripping off her hoodie and handing it to Jonah.

He took the fabric. "Logan, help me. I don't have the strength to hold pressure."

Logan stepped up and used his weight to press against Mallory's side. Jonah couldn't allow himself to think Mallory might not make it. He had faith in God and in Mallory's own will to live.

The paramedics arrived and shoved him aside in order to assess Mallory.

"He's injured, too," Kate said, pointing at Jonah.

"I'm fine. Take care of Mallory first," he insisted.

The paramedic brushed away his concern. "We have two teams here and more on the way so stop playing hero. You're girlfriend is being well cared for. What happened?"

He craned his neck, trying to see what

was going on with Mallory. "She's been stabbed," he called out. "There's a knife wound in her right side."

"Buddy, I'm trying to help you here," the paramedic said, clearly exasperated. "I need to know what happened to you."

"Cracked ribs, maybe broken now," he reluctantly admitted. "And a surgical incision that may have opened up again."

"Where does it hurt? Here?" The paramedic pressed against his lower left side.

Excruciating pain shot through his chest. Despite his best efforts to battle the pain, Jonah passed out cold.

When Jonah awoke, he was already in the hospital. He didn't remember anything about the ambulance ride, which made him wonder if the guy had given him something to knock him out.

He turned his head on the gurney but didn't see Mallory. "Where's Mallory?" he asked the nurse.

She turned toward him. "Hello, my name is Susan. How are you feeling?"

"Fine. Where's Mallory? Mallory Roth?"

"Calm down," she urged, putting a hand on his arm. "I don't know who Mallory Roth is, but I'll try to find out, okay?"

"Logan!" he bellowed, annoyed with the nurse who was trying to placate him.

"Excuse me, ma'am," Logan said, appearing in the doorway to his room. He flashed his badge for the nurse. "I'm with the FBI and I need to talk to this witness."

"Fine. But you need to keep him calm. We just reinflated his lung and repaired the surgical incision he did his best to ruin."

"I promise I'll keep him calm," Logan drawled, flashing his most charming grin.

"Where's Mallory?" he asked, unable to concentrate on anything else until he knew she was okay. "Have you seen her?"

"Mallory is fine. She has a minor concussion and they've already stitched up the wound in her side. They're giving her a couple units of blood to replace what she lost."

"She went to surgery?" He was appalled to know that she'd undergone surgery while he was unconscious.

"No, they took care of everything right in the trauma room," Logan assured him. "I swear to you, she's fine. Resting for now and waiting for a hospital bed. They want to watch her overnight to make sure her head injury doesn't get worse."

He saw the truth in Logan's eyes and allowed himself to relax. Mallory was alive. She was going to be okay.

Thank You, Lord.

"I want to see her," Jonah said. He put a hand to his chest, feeling the bulky dressing along his left side. "Help me up."

"No way, not until the doctor gives the okay."

"I'm fine," he insisted. The pain was bad, but he didn't care. He wanted to see Mallory.

"Knock it off, Jonah," Logan said in an exasperated tone. "One of your broken ribs punctured a lung, and so help me, if you don't stay put, I will help hold you down while that nurse gives you a sedative."

Jonah glared at Logan, but his colleague didn't back down. He ground his teeth in frustration. "Then get the doctor in here to clear me. I doubt I'll need a hospital bed."

"Don't count on that," Logan muttered drily. "Listen, it's time for me to report all this, so humor me for a minute, okay? As soon as you've answered my questions, I'll get the doctor in here."

He narrowed his gaze but he nodded. "Fine. Ask your questions."

"How did you know the warehouse was going to blow up?" Logan asked. "I wanted to get the car, but you made us run in the opposite direction. If we'd have gone to the car, we'd all be dead."

Despite the pain, he flashed a crooked grin. "Chief Ramsey didn't seem to know the place was wired with dynamite, since he showed up with a gun. But Caruso had a knife. I suspected there was a possibility he might be planning to double-cross the chief by blowing all of us up with the warehouse once he had the bracelet. When he was trying to get up but collapsed onto his stomach, he reached for his pocket and I was afraid that he might trigger the explosion by accident, so I wanted to put as much time and distance between us and the warehouse as possible." Thankfully, God had guided him in the right direction.

"But how did you know Caruso was the one who'd wired the warehouse in the first place?" Logan persisted.

Now Jonah understood what was bothering Logan. Logan was the one who'd suggested the warehouse as a meeting place and he couldn't understand how it had been used against them. "You'll have to help me answer that one, Logan. You mentioned you had a contact who told you about the warehouse. Is it possible your contact planned on double-crossing you, too?"

"Bruce Dunlop," Logan said with disgust. "We sent him to work undercover in Salvatore's business. He's the one who gave me the idea of using that particular warehouse and he's the one who was supposed to be helping us from the inside."

Jonah shook his head. "Plenty of guilt to go around, Logan. I'm the one who left the message with Finley telling him we wanted to meet him at the warehouse in the first place."

"No matter when you told Finley the meeting spot, he would have told the chief anyway, to keep him in the loop."

Maybe, but by then they wouldn't have been trapped inside with the chief holding a gun on them. Jonah hated the way he'd made so many mistakes. "You were right, Logan. I should've considered the possibility that the corruption went higher than Finley."

"It's all over now, Jonah. We made it out alive. Unfortunately, both the chief and Caruso died in the explosion."

Jonah nodded. "Yeah, and I still don't know for sure if Finley is dirty, too. I'd like to think not, since the chief showed up without him, but let your boss know so that there can be a full investigation."

"You got it," Logan agreed. He held out his hand and Jonah solemnly clasped it. "Thanks, Jonah. I'll be in touch. And

I'll get the doctor to come in and talk to you now."

"Thanks."

The doctor insisted on admitting him to a hospital bed, and he agreed only if he could be on the same floor as Mallory.

It was several hours later before he was settled in his room on the third-floor surgical unit. Getting out of bed with the IV pump and all his tubing wasn't easy. But he insisted on walking in the hall, so the nurse and the aide reluctantly helped to disconnect him.

"You can't stay off the suction too long," the nurse warned him. "We need to make sure your lung doesn't collapse again, okay?"

Since he didn't particularly want that, either, he nodded. "Just a few minutes. I promise."

With the IV pole in tow, he made his way out to the main nursing station. He found Mallory's room number, inwardly groaning as he realized she was on the opposite side of the floor.

Walking wasn't bad as long as he didn't breathe too much. When he reached Mallory's room the door was closed. He lightly tapped.

"Come in."

He pushed open the door. She was lying in bed, looking pretty good except for the blood dripping through her IV and the dark bruises shadowing her eyes. He crossed the room toward her.

"Jonah!" She looked happy to see him. "Are you okay?"

"Yeah, I'm fine. Just need to make sure my lung stays good, and if it does, they'll take this chest tube out tomorrow morning and let me go home." They'd mentioned the possibility of needing more IV antibiotics but he was sure he could convince them to give him pills instead.

She reached out her hand toward him and he gingerly sat in the chair next to her bed so he could grasp it without too much pain. "Jonah, I'm glad you're here. God has answered my prayers. I was so worried about you."

"I was praying for your safety, too. But I wasn't the one who had surgery in the trauma bay," he pointed out.

"Not true. Logan told me that you had minor surgery but that you were insisting on going home."

"The doctor wouldn't let me. They agreed to put me on the same floor as you so I decided not to argue." Her hand felt so dainty in his, but he knew Mallory was so much stronger than she looked. The blood transfusions had brought color back to her cheeks, and aside from the bruising, she looked great. He silently thanked the Lord again for keeping her safe. "How's your head?"

"Hurts," she admitted. "I feel sick to my stomach, too, but that could be just from seeing the blood." She kept her gaze on his face, and he realized she didn't like watching the blood transfusion drip into her arm. "Can't wait till this one is finished."

He grinned and gently squeezed her hand in reassurance. "It's all over, Mallory. Caruso can't hurt you anymore. I'm sure we'll get a search warrant to go through his house and garage. We'll find out what happened to Claire Richmond. You're free to go home once you're released from the hospital."

"And what about you, Jonah?" she asked, her gaze serious. "Will I ever see you again?"

He stared into her blue eyes and knew the best thing for her would be for him to walk away. Cops weren't a good bet in relationships. His own fiancée had walked away—what if Mallory eventually did the same thing?

She deserved better than a wounded warrior.

"I'm sure we'll see each other again," he said slowly, sidestepping the real meaning of her question. "But for right now, I think you should call your sister. I know Alyssa will want to be here for you."

"She's on her way." Mallory stared at him for a long moment, her gaze full of hurt.

He needed to get out of here, and soon, or he'd change his mind. Time to let Mallory go, so she could move on with her life.

"I better get back to my room," he said finally. He had to drop her hand so he could hold on to his injured side as he stood. "The nurses warned me that I need to keep this chest tube hooked up to suction until tomorrow."

"I understand," she murmured, although her puzzled expression tore his heart. He clamped his jaw shut and pushed the IV pole toward the door.

"Jonah?" she called out, stopping him before he could open the door.

Steeling his resolve, he turned back to her. "Yes?"

"Thanks for showing me the way to our Lord," she said humbly. "Believing in Him has helped me work through my past. I never trusted men, but I want you to know I trust you. I trust that someday, you'll come back to see me. And I want you to know I'll be waiting for you. Because I love you."

He stared at her, feeling as if she'd sucker punched him in the gut. He struggled to breathe without hurting himself. "Mallory, you don't have to say that. You have a concussion. We've been through a lot over this past week and sometimes emotions run high—" He forced the words out, even though he desperately wanted to believe she did know her true feelings.

Her smile was sad. "Jonah, please don't belittle how I feel. I would never say something I didn't mean, although I certainly understand if you don't feel the same way. I—I know that I'm not the sort of woman a man like you might want to become involved with. But that doesn't change how I feel. I love you. And I want you to promise me you'll take care of yourself, okay?"

He wheeled his IV pump around and came back over to her bedside. He couldn't possibly let her believe that he was walking away because of what happened to her. "Listen to me. This isn't about you and your past. I care about you, far more than you can possibly realize. But you don't have any idea what it means to be with a cop. The stress of the job puts a huge strain on our relationships. Our loved ones watch the news in terror. It's not fair to you, Mallory. Now that you've found God, I'm sure you'll find another man to care for."

The last sentence almost got stuck in his throat. Because he didn't want her to find someone else. He wanted her. He loved her. He loved her!

How could he have been such a fool? All this time, he'd acted as if he was protecting Mallory from being with him, when in reality, he was protecting himself. Protecting his heart from being hurt the way he'd been when his fiancée walked away.

Surely if Mallory could overcome her fears, he could do the same?

"You're dooming our relationship before even giving us a chance. Yes, your job is dangerous. But I can't believe there aren't police officers out there who manage to make a relationship work."

She was right about that. There were a few cops who had faith and somehow their marriages survived. "Some, yes, but it's an uphill battle."

"Maybe it is, but isn't that where our faith is supposed to help us? Weren't you the one to convince me that God's strength helps us to shoulder our burdens? I thought you were a true believer."

He thought so, too. But hadn't he known for a while now that God had brought Mallory into his life to strengthen his own faith? She was thanking him for showing her the way to their Lord, when he should be thanking her.

She was the best thing to happen to him, and now that he'd faced his deepest fears, he couldn't let her go. He lowered himself gingerly back into the chair beside her bed and reached over to take her hand again. "You're right, Mallory. I have a confession to make. I love you. I love you so much, it scares me. I feel like I don't deserve such a precious gift."

Her beautiful blue eyes filled with tears. "Crazy man, we both deserve this precious gift of love. God loves us just the way we are. Which means He'll watch over us and protect us, too."

Jonah couldn't find the words to respond, so he simply reached over and kissed her, vowing to make sure she never regretted loving him.

EPILOGUE

Mallory stood next to Alyssa in the back dressing room of the church, amazed that the wedding gowns they'd chosen were so similar in style. Once they'd dressed completely opposite, but not anymore.

"Are you ready?" Alyssa asked.

Mallory nodded, hoping and praying she wouldn't start crying like a baby, ruining her makeup. Because if she started crying, Alyssa would, too. And then they'd both be blubbering idiots walking down the aisle.

The double wedding had been Alyssa's idea, and Mallory was secretly relieved she didn't have to walk down the aisle alone. They'd agreed that since their parents were gone, they would walk together to the church altar. Gage would be waiting on the left side of the church, and Jonah would be waiting on the right.

"I love you, Alyssa," Mallory said. "Thanks for always being there for me."

"Likewise, Mallory," Alyssa said with a tremulous smile. "Now, don't get too mushy on me or we'll both be crying on a day we should be rejoicing."

"I'm happy," Mallory insisted, although she could feel the threat of tears pricking her eyes. "Truly happy."

"Me, too." Alyssa linked her arm with Mallory's. "Come on, they're playing our song."

Mallory took a deep breath and nodded. Together, they left the dressing room and approached the aisle. The church was surprisingly packed with family and friends. Mallory couldn't get over how easily the members had welcomed her into their community.

They paused at the end of the aisle and she smiled when she saw Jonah staring at her in awe. Gage had a similar expression on his face, and she knew in that moment, she and Alyssa were the luckiest women on earth to find two guys like Gage Drummond and Jonah Stewart.

She smiled at Jonah, keeping her gaze locked on his, determined to show him just how much she loved him. Jonah's smile held her steady as she approached the altar. He surprised her by stepping forward to meet her, taking her hand in his. "You look beautiful, Mallory," he murmured.

Her heart swelled with love as they turned to face the pastor. As they recited their vows, she knew there was nothing on this earth that would keep them apart.

* * * * *

Dear Reader,

I've always been fascinated by twins, especially identical twins. I've seen TV documentaries about twins separated at birth who have the same careers, the same medical problems, even the same hobbies. But what if you had identical twins with completely different personalities?

Alyssa and Mallory are twins, but due to a traumatic event when Mallory was younger, they lead very different lifestyles. Until danger forces them to take each other's personalities.

You met Alyssa and Gage in *Identity Crisis*. *Twin Peril* is Mallory and Jonah's story. Mallory is running for her life and doesn't trust men, until she meets Jonah Stewart, a Milwaukee police detective. Jonah knows better than to get emotionally involved with a potential witness, but he can't help responding to Mallory, anxious to help her find faith in God.

Forgiveness is the theme of *Twin Peril* and I hope you enjoy Mallory's story. I'm always thrilled to hear from my readers and I can be reached through my website at www.laurascottbooks.com.

Yours in faith,
Laura Scott

Questions for Discussion

1. In the beginning of the story, Mallory has trouble believing Jonah is there to help her. Discuss a time when you've had trouble believing the best about someone.

2. Jonah not only failed his partner in the past, but his failure was captured on the national news. Discuss a time when you failed someone you cared about in a public way.

3. Mallory has trouble trusting men. Given her past, do you think her issues with trust are justified?

4. Mallory is struggling with forgiving herself for what happened in the past. Discuss a time when you've had trouble with forgiving yourself for something you did.

5. Early in the story, Mallory is afraid to pray because she doesn't know how

and doesn't think God will listen to her if she does. Discuss whether or not you think God would listen to a nonbeliever's attempt to pray.

6. As Mallory and Jonah run away from the burning motel, Mallory begins to pray. Discuss the time when you first began to pray and how that may have changed your perspective on faith.

7. Jonah tells Mallory that God can help us carry our burdens. Describe a time when you used God's help to carry a heavy emotional burden.

8. At one point in the story, Mallory takes Jonah's car keys and attempts to escape. Discuss the emotional turmoil that led to this impulsive decision.

9. Mallory invites herself to go to church with Jonah and then has a panicky moment when she realizes her life is going to change forever.

Discuss a moment when you felt as if you were in a similar situation.

10. Mallory feels acutely guilty for her inadvertent role in Abby's murder. Discuss a moment when you felt as if you were in a similar situation.

11. Toward the end of the story, Jonah refuses to allow Mallory to use herself as bait to draw out Caruso. Discuss the pros and cons of his decision.

12. Jonah believes a relationship with Mallory won't work because the stress of being a cop is too much. Mallory believes faith will get them through the bad times. Discuss a time when faith helped you get through a difficult spot in your relationship.